AMINATA COOTE

A Husband for Christmas

HopeLight Publishers

God decided in advance to adopt us
into his own family by bringing us to
himself through Jesus Christ. This is
what he wanted to do, and it gave him
great pleasure. So we praise God for
the glorious grace he has poured out
on us who belong to his dear Son.

EPHESIANS 1:5-6 NLT

Contents

One

Chapter 1

Mackenzie Porter's stomach rumbled as she put a bottle of cucumber-melon sparkling water on the tray. She placed a hand on her abdomen.

"Easy." She murmured the words under her breath as if soothing an upset child.

"Did you say something?" Lea Young, the hostess who shared her shift, glanced over at her.

She forced a smile. "No." She added a tumbler with three ice cubes to the small tray. "My stomach is a little upset."

"Oh, no." Lea lay a hand on her arm. "Do you want me to take the tray in for him?"

The younger woman's face held a trace of agitation and a bit of awestruck wonder. Mackenzie understood. When she'd first gotten assigned as hostess to Cameron Grant, she'd been more than a little intimidated.

The man was a billionaire whose face and name they often

plastered in the newspapers. Not to mention on several billboards and on magazine covers. Added to that, he was too handsome for any woman's good.

Not that he'd ever brought a woman except his assistant onboard, not while she'd been on shift, anyway. As gorgeous as Cameron was, it was his eyes that were most memorable. The light gray eyes that should be out of place with his dark skin instead had a striking effect.

"I'll be fine." She lifted the tray and smiled at Lea. "Please make a cup of ginger tea for me. I'll drink it when I return."

She paused on the threshold, took a deep breath, and thrust her shoulders back. Showtime. Hostessing for the elite crowd who hired them to serve on their private jets wasn't a demanding job. According to her manager, there were only two requirements—to be pretty and invisible.

Mackenzie glided through the door separating the galley from the main cabin. She kept her eyes fixed on the path she needed to take, rather than allow herself to be distracted by the opulent furnishing of the aircraft.

Cream and black were the dominant colors, and they conveyed both class and elegance. It was like flying in an upscale hotel.

Her stomach gurgled. No. She clenched her teeth against an upsurge as the contents of her stomach battled to free themselves from its confines.

What on earth was going on? She didn't get airsick. Never. Her sister Madison was the one who had trouble flying.

God, give me a few minutes. All I need to do is place the tray on the table beside Mr. Grant and return to the galley. Five minutes. Tops. Please give me five minutes.

She increased her speed as much as possible without appearing rushed. Mr. Grant's head lifted as she approached, his piercing eyes scanning her body. A frown marred his perfect features.

"Are you alright?"

His deep voice usually had her smothering her girlish response. Not today. Why couldn't this have been one of those days when he ignored her?

"Fine."

She dredged up a tight-lipped smile and plunked the tray onto the table beside her. The one worth more than her entire year's salary.

Her father, who owned an antique shop, would be ashamed of her treatment of the priceless artifact. He'd have to forgive her. Her stomach churned, and she pivoted, intent on returning to the galley before her stomach finished its revolt.

"Mackenzie?" Mr. Grant's voice was concerned.

Cameron Grant knew her name? Why was she surprised? She'd only worked with the man for two years.

"Sir?" She resisted the urge to squirm as her stomach rumbled and convulsed. She bit back the taste of bile.

Please, God, get me out of here.

She turned to face the man who sent her a check with a hefty bonus every year. A check she was anticipating more than usual, as she and her siblings had booked a Caribbean cruise for their parents.

Her mouth filled with saliva as the contents of her meal came rushing out of her throat. Mackenzie clapped a hand over her mouth, but it was too late.

Her last meal and everything in her stomach surged upward as the acrid scent of vomit filled her nostrils.

"I'm sorry."

As soon as her stomach stopped heaving, she wheeled away from Mr. Grant and back the way she'd come. Mortification permeated every cell of her body. She had vomited on Cameron Grant. Okay, it had been at his feet, but she was almost certain there had been a splatter on the leg of his trousers.

***

In the crew quarters, Mackenzie rushed past Lea.

"Mackenzie?" The younger hostess followed her. "Are you okay?"

"No." She groaned, clutching her stomach. "Can you clean up for me?"

"What?" Lea screwed up her pretty face.

"I vomited. In the main cabin." On Mr. Grant's foot. Her face burned.

Lea crept closer, concern and shock on her face. "Was he there?"

"Yes." She crawled onto a bed and flung an arm over her face.

"Don't worry about anything," Lea spoke briskly. "You'll soon be fine."

Lea hurried out of the cabin but returned before Mackenzie could wonder where she'd gone. She held a tray bearing a cup of tea and a plate with saltine crackers.

"Sit up."

A rush of gratitude for Lea flowed through Mackenzie. She was glad she had this shift with her instead of one of the other attendants. Some of them would have gloated at her illness. They'd have been scheming ways to use her embarrassment to their benefit. She sat up and took the tray from Lea.

"Thank you."

"Of course." Lea smoothed Mackenzie's hair. "I won't say anything to anyone."

"I didn't think—"

Lea held up a hand. "I've worked with some of the other hostesses. You don't make me feel as if I don't know what I'm doing. Let me help you."

Mackenzie nodded.

Lord, thank You for Lea.

"Drink your tea."

Mackenzie took a sip of tea under Lea's watchful gaze.

"I'll deal with the spill." Lea smiled and slipped through the door.

Lord, I've never been so embarrassed. Why did I have to get sick today? In front of Mr. Grant?

She groaned. How would she live this down? Correction. She'd never live this down. Maybe she'd quit her job. Change her name. Move to a different town. Either way, she never wanted to see Cameron Grant again as long as she lived.

Two

Chapter 2

Cameron Grant's head snapped up when the hostess placed a tray at the table beside him. He squinted at her, eyes flitting to her name tag and then back. "Where's Mackenzie?"

She flinched. "Sir?"

Cameron suppressed a sigh. This was why he preferred working with Mackenzie. She never acted as if she were in awe of him. She made him almost feel normal.

He waved a hand. "You work with Mackenzie, don't you? Where is she?"

The girl's eyes widened. This time, the sigh did escape.

"Never mind." He straightened his bulk out of the chair. "I'll go find her."

Though he didn't understand why he felt the urge to chase after a hostess. Except…the last time she'd worked for him, she'd gotten sick. All over him, to be sure. A pair of pants had almost been ruined.

"Sir."

The attendant, Lea, rushed after him. She darted in front of him as if her slight frame would be enough to bar him from accessing any portion of the plane that he owned. He moved to step past her, but she dashed into his path once again. Hmm. He spared her a glance.

"Is there a reason you're preventing me from speaking with Mackenzie?"

The young woman's face crumpled as if she was on the verge of tears.

"You can't speak to her." Her words were as thin as air.

He scowled. "Is this because of what happened the last time she flew with me?" He made a motion for her to scoot out of the way. "That's ridiculous."

People got sick all the time. Was he some kind of ogre that she thought he'd hold her illness against her?

"She quit."

Cameron rotated his head slowly. "Excuse me?"

Lea dropped her gaze, her body bopping as she shifted from one foot to the next.

"Well, she didn't quit, exactly."

"Explain." He folded his arms over his chest and forced himself to remain as still as possible.

"She..." Lea's eyes flitted to his, then away. "She put in a request to be transferred."

He narrowed his gaze. "Are you saying she doesn't want to work with me anymore?"

Lea swallowed, chin dropping to her chest. "I'm sorry."

A wave of hurt crashed through Cameron. Mackenzie had requested a transfer. Truly, she didn't expect he'd have been angry because of what happened, did she?

Something his friend Levi had said flashed through his mind.

You have these high standards for everyone—requirements no one can meet. You're bound to be disappointed.

He wasn't harsh. Sure, he expected a certain level of professionalism, but that didn't make him a monster, did it?

Cameron studied the woman before him. She trembled with anxiety. Did she expect her job to be in jeopardy because he was angry at Mackenzie's defection? Because he was angry. No, worse. He felt hurt and a little…rejected. What was that about?

Now was not the time to examine his twisted, mixed-up feelings about his long-time hostess. He needed to reassure this one before he had to break in another attendant.

"Lea."

She started, and Cameron gentled his voice.

"Thank you for telling me. I appreciate it."

Her head snapped up as her eyes flew across his face. "You're not mad?"

"No." It was the simplest response and easier to say than trying to explain his tangled-up emotions. "Bring the meal in another hour."

He donned some of the nonchalance he was famous for and headed toward his seat and the report he'd abandoned in pursuit of Mackenzie. This wasn't over. Not by a long shot.

* * *

Cameron tapped his fingers on the polished mahogany surface of the conference table as he listened to the hold music. He'd kept the meeting with his shareholders brief.

For the first time in forever, his mind hadn't been on business. Instead, it had been mulling over the puzzle of Mackenzie's transfer request and how he could get her back.

He had nothing against Lea, but she was as skittish as a colt. When she wasn't jolting and jerking about the cabin, she was staring at him with puppy dog eyes. As for the other attendant they'd assigned to the flight, she'd avoided him the entire time.

The music stopped mid-note and a brusque voice spoke. "What can I do for you, Mr. Grant?"

Calvin Hayes was the manager of the agency that supplied the hostesses for his aircraft. It had taken his secretary, Vivian Ebanks, less than five minutes to track down the man's name and phone number.

"I need the contact information for Mackenzie Porter. Her address would be helpful if you have it."

There was a long pause on the other end of the line. Cameron remained silent. Would the man give up the information? He'd found that sometimes acting as if you were entitled to something was enough for people to give it to you.

"Why do you want it?"

"She left something on board and I wanted to make sure she got it."

"Why don't you send it here?"

Why not indeed? Cameron adopted his most bored tone.

"I didn't want to put you out. Besides, I'm sure Ms. Porter would love to get her property back before the holidays."

"Does this have anything to do with her not wanting to work with you? What happened on your last flight together?"

She hadn't told her boss? Well, he wouldn't be the one to spill her secret.

"Nothing." He contemplated saying more, but in the end,

buttoned his lips. "Are you going to give me her information or not?"

Hayes's sigh was long-suffering. "You understand that this is not standard procedure, right?"

"Of course."

The man rattled off an address, which Cameron scrambled to scribble down.

"Appreciate it."

He hung up the phone and stared at the Orange Valley address. Now that he had it, what would he do with it?

Three

Chapter 3

Mackenzie slouched at the kitchen table, using a hand to push the cat-eyed glasses up her nose. After the debacle on her last flight, she'd sought solace in her hometown of Cinnamon Hill.

Her parents had been ecstatic to spend time with her before they left on their trip. A trip Mackenzie was no longer certain she could afford to contribute to. She groaned.

"Are you listening to me?" Madison waved a hand in front of her face.

"Yes."

Madison, her face a mirror of Mackenzie's except for the glasses, smirked at her.

"Okay, no. But if you knew how badly I messed things up, you'd understand why I can't go home."

She hadn't told her sister the full story. She'd only hinted that it was work-related. Mackenzie still squirmed whenever she remembered, and she still hadn't figured out *why* she'd gotten sick.

Madison leaned toward her, a conspiratorial gleam in her eyes. "I may have a solution to that."

Mackenzie was shaking her head before her sister finished her sentence. Madison pretended to pout.

"What was I going to say?"

Mackenzie met her sister's gaze, staring into the brown eyes so much like her own. "I'm not switching places with you."

"Why not?"

"Because we're not teenagers anymore. This is my life and I'm not in the mood to play games with it."

She gestured to herself. Okay, so she didn't exactly resemble a highly paid hostess at the moment, but Mackenzie loved her job. She loved being able to fly to different places for the simple cost of serving for a few hours.

Madison arched a brow. "Who'll figure it out?"

Mackenzie opened her mouth to protest, but Madison continued, counting points off on her fingers. "Mom and Dad are on a cruise for the next two weeks. RJ's on some mission and won't be back until who knows when."

Their older brother, RJ—Robert Junior—was an intelligence officer. The army often sent him on missions to places he couldn't talk about doing things Mackenzie didn't want to speculate about. She said a quick prayer for him, asking God to protect him wherever he was.

"You said you were on vacation and had no plans until after the new year."

A vacation she'd begged for and had only gotten because she'd threatened to quit. Not that she would, or could, afford to. She hated to admit it, but Madison had a point.

Switching places with her twin would give her the mental space to plan her next move. Because the truth of it was, as much as she loved her job, being a hostess was not what she wanted to do for the rest of her life.

It wouldn't be an option in the next few years as she got older and lost the youthful appearance many of their clients went for. Mackenzie refused to be one of those women who did so many surgeries that they almost became plastic. No. Better to take this opportunity to figure out what to do next.

She studied her sister's faux innocent expression and narrowed her eyes. "What's in it for you?"

Madison widened her eyes, laying a hand against her chest. "Why do you assume I'm benefiting from this arrangement? Can't I do something out of the goodness of my heart because I love my sister?"

Mackenzie straightened and folded her arms across her chest.

"Okay, okay." Madison waved a hand. "You don't have to go all schoolmarm on me." She sighed. "I need a break from everything. Mom and Dad are gone. This is the perfect time for me to get away. In Orange Valley, there are no expectations of me whereas here," she lifted a shoulder. "Everyone will expect me to be all happy and upbeat."

Madison's doctor had diagnosed her with PCOS, shattering her dream of someday becoming a mother. Mackenzie reached for Madison's hand. She was a horrible sister. She should have considered that the holiday would be hard for her twin.

"I'm sorry."

Madison's eyes filled before she dashed away the tears. "It's fine."

"Do you want us to go somewhere else?"

Madison's laugh was harsh. "Where? Coming up with my portion for Mom and Dad's trip almost wiped me out."

Her too. Still, she would have taken her sister somewhere, even if it meant maxing out her credit cards.

"I understand if you don't want to. It's fine." Madison grimaced. "I'll deal with it."

"I'll switch with you." The words plopped out of Mackenzie's mouth before she'd considered the implications. Madison's eyes lit up.

"You will?"

"Yeah." Mackenzie nodded, already regretting her decision. "Please tell me you don't have any big jobs lined up."

Because though her father had trained her, it had been a long time since she'd done any restoration work on her own.

"Uh," Madison reached for her phone. "We have a couple of pieces that we're restoring, but those are mostly done and not due until the end of January. Mr. Johnson is to pick up an armoire Dad had refinished before his trip."

Madison lifted her head, eyes gleaming. "You should have seen it, Kenzie. Dad worked a miracle on that piece."

Madison tapped a few times on her phone and angled it toward Mackenzie. The armoire looked as though it had fought in both world wars and survived. Kenzie swiped for the next image and gasped. Her sister spoke the truth. What their father had accomplished was a miracle.

Madison beamed. "Amazing, isn't it?" She glanced back at her phone.

"Oh, there's an auction on the twenty-third that I was supposed to attend. I'll make sure you have all the details, including the pieces we were hoping to acquire and the budget. The holidays are kind of slow."

"Are they slower than usual?"

Madison winced. "Some. But don't worry, we'll be fine."

How could she not worry? The antique shop was responsible for the livelihood of three members of her family. Would they have been more profitable if she hadn't gone off to do her own thing? If she'd insisted that they do more to join the twenty-first century?

Dad had taught all three of them the business. RJ hadn't been interested. He'd only worked to collect his allowance. Madison had taken to restoration as if she'd been born three centuries ago, but it was Mackenzie who'd had a vision of the company's potential. It was she who had ideas for its future.

Her father had refused to make any changes. He'd rebuffed her efforts to create a website for the business. Robert Porter Senior was as entrenched in the past as the pieces he restored.

She'd walked away at his stubbornness, angry that he didn't trust her to use the skills and talents God had given her while he'd embraced her sister's. Excitement thrummed through her.

Maybe this was her chance to show her father what was possible. She'd spend the next two weeks implementing as many of her ideas as she could, proving to her parents once and for all that she could make this business viable.

And then she'd come back home and take up her rightful place in the family business.

Four

Chapter 4

C ameron checked the address on his phone with the number on the gate before him. It was the right place. The pretty teal house with its dark chocolate door reminded him of Mackenzie—warm and bright.

She'd been a spot of color on every flight, something that shone through despite the drab navy uniform he required his team to wear. He snorted. He hadn't spoken to the woman yet, and he'd become fanciful.

Cameron studied the yard. Either Mackenzie had a green thumb and loved gardening or she paid someone to maintain her property. Colors bloomed across the space. Rose pink bougainvilleas, bright yellow hibiscus flowers, and roses in every hue.

Still, he frowned. There was something different. He swiveled his head to check out the nearby houses. Unlike the others on the block, Mackenzie's was unadorned. Funny.

He'd expected Mackenzie to have gone all out for the holidays.

"Come on, Cam. It's not as though you and the woman are friends."

And he was talking to himself. Cameron snapped his mouth shut. He was acting out of character. Because of a woman who probably considered him a walking automated teller machine. Not that he'd ever gotten that vibe from Mackenzie.

She never flirted with him or tried to get him to support one cause or another. She never intimated that he should be generous with his funds or affection—which made his being here ludicrous.

He was about to start the engine of his truck when the curtain at the front window twitched.

Great. Now he *had* to get out and talk to Mackenzie if he didn't want to get stopped by the police on his way out of town. He could already read the headlines. Billionaire pulled over by the cops. That would be the worst thing to happen.

His stocks would plummet, and he'd have to answer a bunch of questions by the police. His mother would accuse him of dragging their family name through the mud.

As if he could do any more damage than his father with his multiple marriages and often public spats and divorces. Even his mother's charity work had not been enough to dilute the effect of his father's affairs. Lucky for him, his investors were more concerned with his knack for investments than with his personal life.

With a sigh, Cameron unfolded himself from the vehicle and made his way up the short cobblestone driveway. He knocked on the door, tucking his hands into his pockets as he waited. How would he explain his presence on Mackenzie Porter's front step?

Before he got the chance to rehearse his answer, the door drew open, and Mackenzie peered around its edges.

"Yes?"

He'd take the direct approach. "May I come in?"

She examined him from head to toe before releasing an impatient sigh, stepping back for him to enter the house.

He scanned the entry hall, surprised by the antique clock that presided over the small space. Someone had restored the grandfather clock and shone it until it gleamed.

His gaze panned Mackenzie from head to toe. Her yoga pants, spaghetti strap blouse, and messy ponytail were the opposite of the polished woman he was used to. He frowned. Was that why she seemed different?

Mackenzie folded her arms across her chest and tapped her foot. "Well?"

"Do you know why I'm here?"

Her eyebrows shot up. "Why would I know that?"

Why indeed? Cameron studied the woman in front of him. His instincts told him something was off and Cameron was a man who'd learned to follow his gut.

He changed tactics, skewering her with a gaze people had called smoldering.

"You don't?" He pressed into her personal space, towering over her. "Ever since that kiss we shared on your last shift, I can't stop dreaming about you."

Her eyes widened as she raised both hands to fend him off. "Mr. Grant!"

Cameron backed up. "So you do know who I am."

He studied her face. What would she do next?

"Yes, Mr. Grant. I've been working for you for the past eighteen months."

He arched a brow. Two years, but who was counting?

"Look." The Mackenzie imposter swiped a hand over her hair. "I shouldn't have kissed you." She took a deep breath. "It was unprofessional and I'm sorry. I hope you won't hold it against me and it won't affect our relationship."

She took a step back. Was she afraid of him?

"So, you admit we have a relationship?" He gave her a cocky smile, testing how far she'd go to keep up the charade.

"A professional one." She raised a hand. "You and I have a professional relationship that will remain that way."

Okay, as much as he enjoyed her being flustered, enough was enough. "Who are you and what have you done with Mackenzie?"

She sputtered. "Nothing." Her eyes widened. "I mean, I'm Mackenzie." She patted her chest. "Mackenzie Porter, that's who I am." She straightened to her full unimpressive height of five feet ten inches. "You should leave, Mr. Grant."

"Gladly."

He pivoted. He had more questions than answers. On his way out, his eyes caught on a collage that hung beside the door. Most of them were of Mackenzie, but in one photo, there were two of them.

He should have guessed. Twins. But how could he figure out where Mackenzie's twin was supposed to be? Because if she was here, he would bet Mackenzie was where her sister should have been. And he wasn't a betting man.

He rested a palm on the doorjamb. "Mackenzie?"

"Hmm?"

"What's your sister's name?"

"Madison."

Cameron bit back a grin. If he located Madison Porter, he'd

find his missing Mackenzie.

A text message to his IT manager and a brief, impatient wait were all it took for Cameron to have a name and an address. Madison Porter worked at Forever Furnished, an antique store in Cinnamon Hill. That explained the clock in the hall.

He searched for the store online. Nothing. Did they still have brick-and-mortar stores that didn't have an online presence? He called his assistant.

"Vivian." He wasted no time when she answered. "Cancel all my appointments for the next two weeks. And find me someplace to stay in Cinnamon Hill. I don't care where, as long as it's private and I won't have a bunch of people ogling me."

"Yes, sir."

"And Vivian?" He waited until she responded.

"Yes?"

"Tell no one where I'm at. Not my mother, not my father." Especially not them.

"Yes, sir. I'll contact you when I find a place for you to stay." There was a pause. "Will you need clothes?"

"If you can get some to me without alerting anyone. Casual wear only."

"Of course, sir."

If he was on vacation, he would dress the way he wanted to.

Five

Chapter 5

Mackenzie surveyed the shop floor, hands propped on her hips. The showroom was so cluttered she wasn't sure it could still be called that. It would take the entire two weeks to organize the space. She blew out a breath. This was something she wanted to do.

"Alright, Mackenzie," she said aloud. "Approach this in the most logical way."

Her eyes roamed over the place again. Maybe it would help if she started with a vision of what she hoped to accomplish. Then she'd have something to refer to when she veered off-track.

Alright. She glanced toward the front door. Did she have time to dart into her father's office for paper and something to write with?

She gnawed at her lip. Should she lock the door? She glanced at the door and then toward the office. It's not as if the place was bustling with customers. In the three hours since she'd opened the shop, she'd had one call. A wrong number.

The guy had been trying to reach the flower shop. She wouldn't speculate about why he needed to buy flowers that early in the morning. It was almost Christmas, after all.

Decision made, she dashed toward the office with one more peek over her shoulder. It would be fine. Sure, there were several valuable items in the store, but a thief would need lots of determination and time to uncover them. She'd be back in a jiffy. Her phantom thief wouldn't have time to discover the first gem.

Five minutes. It had taken that long to locate a sheet of paper. And it was the back of an old invoice from five years ago. She shook her head. Her dad must be in charge of the showroom. Why was he doing that and not her mom? She had no clue.

Or maybe she did. Her father didn't understand the meaning of the word delegation. He would rather leave a task undone than have someone else touch it. He had probably banned anyone from making any changes without his permission. She sighed.

Lord, please help Dad recognize he needs to let us help him.

She sat at the sturdy desk that also held the manual cash register. She scowled at it. It needed to go. This may be an antique store, but that didn't mean they couldn't make use of technology.

"Must have done something awful for you to glare at it that way."

She recognized that voice. Mackenzie's head snapped up. She gasped. What was Cameron Grant doing here? He wore a pair of dark jeans and a navy blue pullover sweater with a zipper on the front. The sweater clung to him in a way his business suits never had and her mouth went dry. What was wrong with her?

She tucked a strand of hair behind her ear. She never acted like this over him. Sure, he was gorgeous, but he was so far out of her league, he may as well be in another universe. Her heart pounded as if she'd run a mile. Why was he here? Not only in Cinnamon Hill but in her family's antique shop?

Would he recognize her? After all, she appeared nothing like the polished version of herself that she always presented. Besides, there were the glasses. It had worked for Superman and his alter ego.

His brow furrowed as he stared at her.

"You look...familiar."

She forced a laugh. "Oh? Maybe I have one of those faces."

"No."

Cameron shook his head, studying her as he moved closer. She held her breath. What was she supposed to do? This was why she hated switching places with Madison. She was never sure how to act when people mistook her for her twin.

"I figured it out." He snapped his fingers. "My attendant Mackenzie is the spitting image of you."

She stiffened before forcing a laugh. "Oh, you've met my sister, Mackenzie. I'm her twin, Madison." Disappointment flashed across his face, then disappeared.

She smiled brightly. "How may I help you?"

Should she pretend she didn't recognize him? No, everyone who lived on Saturn Island knew who he was. He'd consider her an idiot if she did that.

"Mackenzie had a twin?"

She kept her smile in place. Why was he pretending they'd been friends? Why was he here?

He clasped his hands behind his back, eyes roaming around the space. How did this place appear through his eyes? She suppressed a wince.

She needed to get things shifted around to make it easier for potential customers to identify what they sold. If she had her way, Forever Furnished would do more than the occasional restoration project. They'd be the name everyone considered when they wanted to purchase quality antique pieces.

"Uhm," he shook his head. "What exactly do you do here?"

Her cheeks warmed. Wait…

"If you don't know what we do, why did you come in?"

Mackenzie straightened her back, feeling a boldness to speak to her former client that she wouldn't have had when she'd been herself.

He arched a brow. "Someone recommended your store, but now that I'm here," his gaze roamed around the cluttered space. "I'm not sure if they gave me the correct information."

Mackenzie suppressed a sigh. She'd have been confused, too. This was why her family needed her to play a more active role in the business.

"We restore old furniture." Please don't let him have some old antique piece that needs restoring. She was not Madison. Mackenzie's skills in that area were rudimentary. She clasped her hands. "We also sell antique pieces."

"Do you have any pieces available for sale?"

"Uh…"

Why hadn't she gotten a list of the inventory? Did such a list exist? His gray eyes met hers, a trace of amusement in them. Was he laughing at her? He would not get the better of her.

She tilted her chin. "Were you searching for something in particular?"

"Well," he stroked his chin. "I need some pieces to furnish a room."

Yes. This was the type of job they needed. If she did a great job, maybe Cameron would recommend their services to other people in his circle. She frowned.

"Who did you say had recommended us to you?"

He waved a hand. "I don't recall."

She frowned at him. She found that hard to believe. He smirked.

"Did you assume I was strolling through the neighborhood, expecting to find someone who resembles a former employee?"

When he said it that way, she felt like a fool. Especially since she'd requested a transfer without giving him a hint of her intentions.

"Of course not." Mackenzie swiped her hand on her skirt under the desk. "If you had nothing specific in mind, we could attend a few auctions, maybe some rummage sales to see if anything grabs your attention."

Great going, Mackenzie. You invited a billionaire to go to rummage sales with you. As if he'd have the time. Or the desire to go anywhere with her. And what would happen if a reporter or some random person took a picture of them together?

Although dressed as he was, you could almost mistake him for a normal person. An extraordinarily handsome one, but still. A smile teased at the corner of his lips. How had she considered him stern? The smile changed everything. Including, apparently, her traitorous heart's ability to remain aloof.

"I'm sorry." She rushed to cover her mistake. "I shouldn't have assumed you'd have the time to slum around with me. Or that you'd want to."

What was wrong with her? She'd never have spoken to Cameron Grant like this when she'd been Mackenzie Porter. She almost rolled her eyes. Silly girl, you're still Mackenzie Porter.

"I'd be happy to work with your assistant or whoever you have overseeing this project."

"As it happens, I have a couple of weeks off. Choosing the furniture for this project may be an interesting way to spend the holidays."

Mackenzie held back a scream. Cameron Grant had agreed to spend the holiday with her. On business. She needed to sear that into her memory. Because she wouldn't be another woman who lost her head—or her heart—over Cameron Grant.

No, this was a way for her to boost her family's business and also carve out a place for herself. Nothing more. Nothing less.

Six

Chapter 6

Cameron left the antique shop in a daze. He'd confirmed that Mackenzie and her sister had switched places, but not the reason for it. Did it have anything to do with her getting sick the last time she'd flown with him?

Cameron hopped into his truck and slumped his head against the headrest. He'd started this quest because he'd wanted an explanation for why she'd refused to work with him anymore. He'd wanted to explain that he hadn't been angry because of the whole vomiting thing. She'd gotten sick. It was understandable.

True, a part of the reason he'd sought her out had been selfish. He enjoyed working with Mackenzie. She anticipated his needs as only his assistant did, and Vivian had been working with him for over ten years. He hadn't wanted to lose Mackenzie as an employee.

He'd kept going out of curiosity. Why had the sisters switched places? And how could he get them to admit it?

Cameron was used to the spark of attraction when he was around her—a low buzz of electricity reminding him he was alive, and that she was a beautiful woman.

But what had happened inside went beyond that. He'd taken one look at Mackenzie and his gut had tangled up. Without her makeup and the sleek hairstyle she favored when onboard, she was a cross between the girl next door and a sexy librarian.

How was a man supposed to bear up under that kind of pressure? He needed help. Cameron speed-dialed Levi.

"I'm stalking an employee." He blurted out the words the second his friend answered. There was a pause on the other end of the line before Levi spoke.

"You're aware that I have connections in law enforcement, right?"

Levi Armstrong was a firefighter and his oldest friend. They'd met at a youth camp when his parents had sent him away to pursue their own hobbies and had been friends ever since. Somehow, they'd maintained their friendship over the years.

"Should I send the cops after you?"

"Ha-ha."

Levi chuckled. "Why don't you tell me the full story?"

He did. "I'm attracted to her."

"Yeah?"

"I want to ask her out."

Levi's curiosity thrummed over the phone. His desire to pursue his attraction to Mackenzie was as much a surprise to him as it was to his friend. Since Cameron had taken over the running of his family's real estate development firm, he'd spared no time for romantic entanglements. Especially after what had happened five years ago.

"Maybe I should come meet this woman."

"You could. Vivian got me a three-bedroom house." Did she truly believe he needed that much room? Was he high maintenance?

"I'll consider it."

Cameron put the phone on speaker and texted the details to Levi.

"Tell me if you can get away."

"Yeah. This is most likely redundant, but now's the time to lean into the Word. The enemy likes to find little footholds in our lives and turn them into strongholds."

Levi had a point. Because since he'd learned Mackenzie hadn't been on his last flight, Cameron hadn't been acting like himself. The last thing he wanted to do was to give his greatest enemy the ammunition to destroy him.

* * *

Cameron roamed around his temporary home. What was he supposed to do on vacation for two weeks? He'd been working since he was eighteen. When his father had resolved to pursue philandering full-time, his mother had announced he was old enough to take over the business.

He'd worked during the days, eking out time at night to take business classes. He pinched the brow of his nose. Two weeks. That was the amount of vacation time most people got each year and always wanted more. Surely he could entertain himself for fourteen days?

After he figured out what he'd do with the furniture he'd

hired Mackenzie to purchase. He called his assistant.

"Sir?"

"I've hired an antique supplier to buy some items for me."

"Sir?" Vivian drew the word out. "Is there something wrong with Sterling Properties?"

Cameron pinched the brow of his nose. He shouldn't have called Vivian because, of course, she'd be concerned about the real estate firm he'd been using for years to furnish his properties.

"No, this is of a more personal nature."

What was he doing?

"Would you like me to work with this new company?"

"No. I'll take care of it." He strolled over to the window that overlooked the lawn. The view reminded him of Mackenzie's house in Orange Valley. Maybe she'd enjoy this garden.

Cameron shook his head to dislodge the foolish notion. He and Mackenzie had a business relationship. He was her client, and she was his soon-to-be restored hostess. The tingle of awareness had nothing to do with anything.

"Is there—" he blew out a breath. This woman was tangling him up. "Do I have an empty building that needs furnishing?"

"The property you inherited from your uncle last year is still unoccupied. It's a few miles from the house I rented for you. It may not be empty though, since your uncle had been living there at the time of his…until the end."

His uncle Ezra had left him a house when he'd died last year. Cameron had forgotten about it. He hadn't even gone out to the house to check what kind of condition it was in, or the state of its furnishings.

He'd examine it and decide if the place was worth keeping and, if not, what he was going to do about it.

"Send me the details." Could he convince Mackenzie to help him with that task? Why was he always thinking about her?

"Are you alright, Mr. Grant?"

He dragged his mind back to the conversation. "Yes. Why do you ask?"

"It's just—"

Cameron sighed. Was there something about him that prevented people from being honest with him? He wouldn't have noticed it if not for Mackenzie's behavior today. How she'd interacted with him when she was pretending to be a stranger differed from the way she'd acted in the past two years.

"Vivian, you've worked with me for more than a decade. Why aren't you more comfortable sharing your opinions with me?"

"We don't have that kind of relationship, sir."

Cameron glowered. "How would you describe our relation-ship?"

The dead air on the line went on so long that he didn't expect her to answer.

"The type where you give instructions and expect them to be followed."

He stifled a groan. In other words, he was an ogre.

"Fine." He cleared his throat to remove the gruffness from his voice. "Then I instruct you to tell me why you're concerned."

Glad no one else was there, he rolled his eyes at his inane statement.

Vivian exhaled a sigh that could be categorized as a mild hurricane. "You're acting out of character. You've canceled meetings and taken an unplanned vacation. I've worked with you for a decade and you haven't taken more than a week off.

Total."

Cameron listened, almost surprised his assistant had so much to say. This was the longest conversation he'd ever had with her. Because she was right. He gave her a list of tasks to complete and moved on with his day. Her efficiency had been expected. Taken for granted.

"Is that…" he couldn't believe he was asking this question. "A good thing?"

Another pause.

"I'm not sure," Vivian murmured. "I'll wait to discover what kind of man you become afterward."

Cameron said his goodbyes, her words echoing in his head. He was a fair employer, wasn't he? Cameron treated his employees well. He paid them a competitive wage and ensured that his company offered excellent benefits. They had premium health insurance, a pension with an employer match, and a gym membership.

There was even a scholarship program and an annual staff event. What more could he do?

You have these high standards for everyone—requirements no one can meet. You're bound to be disappointed.

Was he making it difficult for people to succeed? Was that why Mackenzie had quit? Because she feared she hadn't met his impossible-to-meet standards?

Seven

Chapter 7

Mackenzie bent her knees and wrestled with the huge sideboard. The sideboard had intricate carvings along the front.

Sure, it was from the Gothic revival era and had more than a few faces carved into the wood, but it didn't deserve to be buried in the middle of a store. Not when someone could buy it and have it in a place of honor in their home.

If she shifted it a few inches, she could slip behind it and clear the clutter that rested out of reach. Then she'd polish it until it gleamed, showing its true beauty. She'd been up since the wee hours of the morning, in the store before dawn.

So far, she'd de-cluttered one tiny section of the shop floor and, as it was the space closest to the door, she was counting it as a victory. For the first time in maybe decades, passersby could get a glimpse of what Forever Furnished offered.

"Come on, you stupid thing. Move!" She made a mighty

heave.

"Do you always talk to inanimate things?"

Mackenzie spun her head while releasing her hold on the sideboard. Her backward motion continued, and she flailed her arms to stop her motion.

"Whoa. I've got you."

A deep voice rumbled close to her ear as muscular arms enveloped her. He smelled like expensive leather and sunshine. She groaned. What does sunshine smell like, Mackenzie?

"Are you alright?"

"Yes." She pulled away from him. Was she doomed to embarrass herself in front of this man forever?

"How can I help you, Mr. Grant?"

A smile teased at the corner of his lips. Had she ever seen him smile? Suddenly, she wanted to.

"I forgot your name." His expression was sheepish. "And I didn't give you my number yesterday or make plans to follow up on that offer."

She nodded. He was going through with it? She hadn't wanted to put too much faith in his words. After he'd left, she'd convinced herself that he'd taken pity on her because she resembled his former hostess, er, her.

Mackenzie swallowed as the memory swept through her mind. She'd vomited all over his expensive trousers. Would he request her dismissal? All he had to do was report what had happened and her career as an attendant was over. She swiped her palms against the side of her pants.

"Your name is…?"

Oh. She tittered. She hadn't answered him. "Mack— Madison Porter."

He smirked. "Are you sure?"

"Of course I'm sure." Her eyebrows winged up. She hated lying.

He shrugged. "For a second there, it sounded as if you were going to say, Mackenzie."

His eyes burned into hers. Had he figured out her secret? Her cheeks warmed. He couldn't have. Until yesterday, Cameron Grant didn't know she had a sister, much less a twin. The only persons who'd ever been able to tell them apart were their parents, RJ, and their closest friends.

"Nice to see you again, Mr. Grant. I'm glad you returned—gives us the chance to discuss what your needs are."

She gestured him further into the store toward the desk at the back. The location wasn't ideal.

Why should their customers have to come all the way into the back of the store to speak with them or to cash out their purchases? The cash register and desk should be closer to the front. She added it to her mental to-do list.

He didn't budge. Cameron stuck a thumb over his shoulder. "What were you trying to do?"

She glared at the offending sideboard. "Move it."

"By yourself?"

He scanned her from head to toe, his smirk becoming a full-on grin. Had she wanted him to smile? She changed her mind because Cameron Grant, with a smile on his face, was devastating. His features lightened and made him more approachable.

"Yes, well," she cleared her throat, tilting her head at a slight angle. "God didn't build all of us like bears."

He chuckled at her words, and she resisted the urge to cover her face with her hands. Why had she developed verbal diarrhea around him? She'd never had the urge to speak this freely with him before.

"Maybe not." He flexed, causing his shoulder muscles to jump. Be still her heart. "But this bear is helping you with your task. Where did you want it?"

"It's fine." She lifted a hand. "I'll get someone to help me with it later."

"Don't be silly. You need help and I'm here now."

"Fine." She chomped off the word. "You can move it to that spot." She pointed to an area about three feet away from its current location.

Lord, why did You send Cameron Grant to terrorize me?

He moved the sideboard without breaking a sweat. Mackenzie's conscience pricked her for her uncharitable thought. Mr. Grant was a client—one doing manual labor for her when she was the one who was supposed to be helping him.

"Thanks, Mr. Grant."

"Please," he smiled down at her. "Call me Cameron."

Mackenzie blinked. Two, no, three smiles in less than fifteen minutes? What was wrong with him? Call him Cameron? She gritted her teeth against the anger that swelled in her chest.

She'd worked with him for two years and he'd never made her that offer. Yet, after two brief conversations with Madison, he was on a first-name basis with her? She scowled at him.

What did Madison have that she didn't? They were identical twins. Was it because he hadn't hired Madison to serve meals and to attend to his comfort? Was that it?

She ignored the rational part of her brain. The part that reminded her he still hadn't met Madison as she was the same person he'd interacted with for those two years.

Her anger increased. Why did her being here make him act differently?

"Have I upset you?"

She blinked, clearing her features. "No. Why do you ask?"

"You're glaring at me."

She plastered on her biggest fake smile. She couldn't afford to alienate him. Not before she'd impressed him with her ability to find the perfect antique pieces for his property.

"You haven't upset me."

"No?" Cameron folded his impressive arms across his chest. "Then why are you always frowning at me?" His eyes bore into hers.

Oh, brother. How would she explain her antagonistic behavior toward him?

The truth will set you free.

She flung her arms up. "I'm embarrassed."

His brow furrowed. "Why?"

So many reasons, not all of which would make sense to him. "You always catch me when I'm talking to myself."

His eyes softened. "It's cute."

Mackenzie's cheeks warmed. He thought she was cute? Butterflies fluttered in her stomach. Wait, was he talking about her, or did he mean *Madison* was cute?

This was why she hated pretending to be her twin. Switching places made her brain hurt.

Eight

Chapter 8

⁓ ∾⚬∽⚬∾ ⁓

Cameron got comfortable across from Mackenzie. It may be perverse of him, but her unsettlement amused him. He'd examine his motives later. For now, he was content to stare at her. She was still wearing her librarian glasses. This time, her hair was in a bun.

He wanted to loosen it until her hair swung free around her shoulders. Better yet, he wanted to kiss her until she lost that buttoned-up look. He shook his head to dislodge the thought. Time to focus on the business at hand. Something that never used to be hard for him.

"I need to amend my request."

His gut clenched at the disappointment in her eyes.

"Oh?"

"Yesterday, I asked you to furnish a room for me." He leaned back in his chair. He'd found that he got more people to agree with his demands when it didn't appear as if he cared about the result.

"I've changed my mind. Some time ago, I inherited a property that I still haven't gone through. I need someone to go through the items in the house with me to determine if there's anything of value. Then," he shrugged. "I may need to sell a few pieces and buy others."

Cameron met her gaze. "If there are any valuable pieces that I decide to sell, there'd be a finder's fee in it for you."

Mackenzie nibbled at her bottom lip. "Do you have any idea what kind of furniture is in the house?"

"No." He hadn't been to Ezra's home since he'd been a child, which was why it had surprised him when his uncle had left the house to him.

"Hmm," she tapped a pattern on the desk.

"I'd pay you, of course."

She quirked a brow at him. "What you need is a cleaning crew, Mr. Grant, not an antique dealer or restorer."

"Didn't I ask you to call me Cameron?"

Her nostrils flared. "As enticing as the idea of cleaning your house may be to some people, Mr. Grant, I have to decline." She stood.

Cameron cocked his head. She'd turned him down? How was it that this woman who had no experience with negotiations had refused him?

"If there's nothing else…"

"I'm willing to do an exchange."

"What do you mean?"

He swiveled his head to encompass the messy room.

"If you help me clean up my uncle's house, I'll help you rearrange this store." He flexed his muscles, feeling a rush of pleasure when her eyes dropped to his chest.

She squinted at him in suspicion. "What's the catch?"

He adopted his most innocent expression. "No catch. I want your help and you need someone to move stuff for you. This will be to our mutual benefit."

She dropped back into the chair and studied him. Cameron concentrated on keeping his breath even and not squirming under her scrutiny.

"Why me?"

Because he wanted to spend enough time with her for this attraction to burn itself out of his system. Because he wanted to get close enough for her to admit she'd switched places with her sister. To find out why she'd requested a transfer, and to beg her to reconsider. He was worse than an ogre—he was a selfish beast.

"I need this place cleaned out and I have a limited time to do it. You're in a similar position." He lifted a brow. "Am I right?"

She gave a tiny nod.

"What harm could come from us helping each other?"

She wrinkled her nose. "Something tells me I'll regret this."

"Then we have a deal?"

Uncertainty swirled in her eyes. "I guess."

He held out a hand. She grabbed it and electricity shot up his arm. What kind of magic was this? His eyes flew to hers. Did she feel it, too? What was he supposed to do about it?

God, why am I attracted to the one woman who wants nothing to do with me?

He drew back his hand and cleared his throat.

"I have a few hours. Later, we'll create a schedule."

That's right, Cameron. Focus on the business. Not how beautiful she was with her lips parted and that dazed expression in her eyes.

"Yes, well, okay." Her tongue darted out to moisten her lips, and he stifled a groan. "That works. Let me show you what needs to be moved."

* * *

Mackenzie had a penchant for music from the sixties and seventies. And was determined to work until she dropped, or maybe it was him she wanted to collapse from sheer exhaustion.

Since their agreement, she'd assigned him a steady stream of tasks. Move this there, or over there. It was always a ridiculously heavy piece of furniture that had him yearning to call someone else to have them deal with it.

He grunted after moving the latest item—a mammoth bookcase that weighed as much as the Titanic. And it was empty. How much worse would it be after someone had loaded it up with books?

But this wouldn't do. He'd never get her out of his system if all they did was work. He swiped his brow. Cameron took a moment to study her where she knelt on the floor, sorting through a box filled with yellowed paper, and he didn't want to know what else.

"Do you always listen to old-people music?"

"Excuse me?" Her head snapped up.

He tipped his chin toward the overhead speakers. A smile danced around her lips.

"I don't notice it anymore." She met his gaze. "My father has distinct ideas about what an antique shop should be like. This is the type of music he believes is appropriate."

Her words held a tinge of bitterness.

"Is that why you're doing this on your own?"

She dropped her eyes. "I'm not the best at restoring old pieces. My sister," she grinned. "She's gifted. Give the girl an old can and she'll transform it into a work of art. I've often teased that she was born in the wrong century."

"What's your talent?"

She ruffled the papers in her hand. "My gift is more modern."

Would she volunteer more information without being prodded? After a moment, he prompted. "Meaning?"

She gestured to the store. "Everything should have its place. When they do, they work harder for you than when you stick them where they don't belong."

Cameron rotated his head to take in the store. Though they'd only been at it a few hours, the place looked different. A sleeping damsel who'd shaken off her old garments in favor of new ones.

He shook his head. He needed to get out more. A few hours with Mackenzie-Madison and he'd started sprouting poetry.

"Do you want to get something to eat? I'm starving."

As if on cue, his stomach rumbled. He pointed to his gut. "See?"

She nibbled at her bottom lip, and Cameron forced himself to look away.

"That's not a smart idea."

What was her problem with him?

She stood, dusting off the knees of her dark pants.

"We can stop for today." Her eyes darted away from his. "What's the address of the house you want me to help you with?"

Okay. He'd let her have this win. But he would figure out why she avoided him as if he had the plague—unless he was

being her errand boy. He'd also like to understand why it
bothered him so much.

43

Nine

Chapter 9

Mackenzie hesitated in the overgrown yard. Cameron had inherited Ezra Murray's house? The curmudgeon had been the neighborhood Scrooge when she'd been a child. He'd chased children away from his house, captured any balls that flew into his yard, and refused to return them.

She shook her head. The world was small indeed, and it was amazing how people were connected.

Mackenzie walked up the concrete driveway that kept the overgrowth at bay. She used the brass knocker to announce her arrival. She smoothed a hand over her hair, then dropped it in a hurry.

What was she doing? This wasn't a date. No, this was payment for him helping her yesterday. She'd work for a few hours and then it would be his turn to help her again.

She groaned…just as the door swung open. Cameron arched

a brow at her.

"Are you okay?"

"Fine."

In a perfect world, she'd have sailed past him into the house, leaving him to follow in her footsteps. But the world wasn't perfect and Cameron stood in the doorway, his bulk blocking her entry. No way she'd be able to push past the linebacker-sized man. Not when he towered almost a foot over her.

Did he have to be so handsome? It should be a crime to resemble a model in a pair of jeans and a T-shirt.

"Do you mind?" She gestured to him.

Cameron frowned. "Do you always wake up on the wrong side of the bed, or is this treatment reserved for me?"

She tilted her head to meet his gaze and gave him a sweet smile.

"It's all for you."

He gave a bark of laughter before shifting out of the way. Mackenzie ducked as she brushed past him. She needed to have her head examined. Antagonizing a potential customer was not the way to drum up business. Especially not when that person was Cameron Grant who had enough money to bury her family's tiny antique shop.

"Good to know I'm special to you."

What? She jerked her head to stare at him and froze. His lips quirked in a half-smile as he watched her, the expression in his eyes almost possessive.

He met her eyes and the heat in his had her sucking in a breath before the answering emotion whooshed through her body like wildfire.

What would it be like to touch his face and the smile that danced on his lips? To step into his arms and have him hold her? To kiss him to find out if it was as good as she imagined?

Her tongue darted out to moisten her lips and his eyes dropped to her mouth. Oh no, this would not do. She couldn't be attracted to Cameron Grant.

What would happen if she had to fill in for someone and work for him one day? It had happened before. How would she work with Cameron again if she kissed him?

Besides, why was she considering kissing him when he believed she was Madison? It would be her luck to kiss someone and have it be the best one of her life, and he didn't know who she was.

She tugged the bandana out of the pocket of her slacks and snapped it before refolding it the way she wanted it. The tension broke.

"What are we working on today?" She tied the bandana over her hair.

He closed the door behind him, eyes dancing with amusement.

"Don't you have one of those twelve-step plans that outline every step of this house sorting?"

"Oh, no, General." She smirked at him. "This is your circus, and I defer to your management of it."

He scrubbed a hand over his face. "Please?"

"Aren't you supposed to be some hotshot real estate developer? Isn't this kind of thing your jam?"

"No. I work with blueprints and topical maps. What I do is more conceptual than anything."

"Pretty sure the newspaper had pictures of you at a construction site."

"You read about me?" The smile on his lips teased at her.

Yes. She'd devoured everything she could find out about

the man in printed papers and online. Not that there was much information. The articles she'd read were always about a business deal. Occasionally, they mentioned him when one of his parents made the papers.

She folded her arms across her chest. "I read the newspapers. Is it my fault you're always in them?"

He grinned. "Tell you what, why don't we go through this house room by room and come up with a plan of action? Will that work?"

Cameron wanted her opinion? He wanted to work with her to create a plan? She gave a tiny nod.

"Okay."

"Are you always this quiet, Madison?"

She scowled. "Can you not call me that?"

"What? You don't like your name?"

She loved it. But having him call her by her sister's name was grating on her nerves. Especially when he smiled at her the way he was now—as if he had a secret and she was it.

"What should I call you instead? Or should I just point and grunt when I want your attention?"

She suppressed a snicker. "Call me Noelle."

His eyes ran over her from head to toe. "It suits you."

"Thanks. Do you have…" She moved her hands in a writing motion.

Cameron produced a notepad and pen as if it were a magic trick.

"Where did those come from?"

He hadn't been holding anything when he'd opened the door.

"I realized yesterday that the key to your heart was sta-tionery."

"You tease, but people have accomplished a lot of things with the perfect set of stationery supplies."

"A woman after my own heart." He smiled down at her, and her traitorous heart did a flip. "Why don't we do this thing?"

"Yes, let's." Her voice was more breathy than she'd have liked, but she ignored it. She took a step back, needing to clear her head. She'd been so focused on Cameron that she hadn't paid attention to the house they were in.

Mackenzie took several steps until she was in the center of the nearest room. She spun in a slow circle, taking everything in. Not that there was much visible. Large shapes covered with white fabric dominated the room.

"I had someone cover everything after I inherited the house. I'd planned to do more, but life got in the way."

She drew in a lungful of air. The air was less musky than she'd expected.

"It doesn't smell that bad."

"Water." He pointed to several buckets around the room. "Plus, I opened every window two days ago."

"Why isn't someone doing this for you again?"

He shrugged. "What else am I supposed to do for two weeks while I'm on vacation?"

She snorted at his befuddled tone. "Do what normal people do. Rest. Go to the beach. Read books. Watch movies and too much TV." She shrugged. "The usual stuff."

"Would you do those things with me?" The earnestness in his eyes made her want to commit to all kinds of things. But no, Mackenzie needed to focus on the job at hand.

"Right."

She pivoted and stomped in the other direction, stopping when she came to a wall that had no business being there.

Was Cameron flirting with her? What happened to the

taciturn man she'd worked with for two years? The man who never dated? Was this what he did? Have incognito vacations and flirtations with unsuspecting women?

Her hands curled into fists. Cameron Grant would not make a fool of her. She would not be his holiday fling.

Ten

Chapter 10

Cameron stared after Mackenzie's back. Once again, he'd said the wrong thing. Why did he keep messing up with this woman? And why did it matter to him? He hadn't been this fascinated with her when she'd worked for him. Or rather, he'd been able to bury the glimmer of attraction he'd had for her. He didn't date the women who worked for him. Ever. No matter how attractive they were or how much they wanted him to.

What was different about Mackenzie? Was it because he sensed layers of her personality? Layers he wanted to peel back until he'd uncovered her core.

He dropped the things in his hand on the nearest surface and followed her into his uncle's living room. Mackenzie faced the wall, hands curled into fists at her side.

"Ma—"

She flinched. Maybe he should tell her he was aware of her

twin switch. That he'd known since the beginning. Would that improve the situation or worsen it?

He needed to recover some ground with this woman. Cameron took a deep breath and started again.

"Noelle, I'm sorry if I made you angry. Though I'm not sure what I did this time." Or any of the times before. Why did she hate him? Had she always disliked him? There had been no signs of it before.

"Please," he lifted a hand, stopping short of brushing her shoulders. "Could you look at me?"

She whirled, brown eyes snapping up to his. "Am I a joke to you?"

She propped her hands on her hips. "You met Madison less than two days ago and already you're on a first-name basis with her?"

This was about Madison? Okay, time to let this secret out of the bag.

"Mackenzie."

"I would never have guessed you were the type of person to swoop in and sweet talk a woman if I hadn't witnessed it for myself." She poked him in the chest.

"Mackenzie."

"I thought you were a decent guy, even if you were too handsome for women to keep their heads around you. How could I have been so wrong about you?"

"Mackenzie."

He grabbed her hand. She froze.

"Why do you keep calling me that?"

"That's your name, isn't it? Mackenzie Noelle Porter?"

Her eyes dropped to his chest. "How long have you known?"

"Since I went to Orange Valley and found your sister there."

Her eyes shot to his. "You went to my house?"

"Yes. Madison didn't tell you?"

Mackenzie shook her head. He'd assumed as much.

"How did you figure it out?"

"Hmm. Funny thing about that." He moved his thumb in lazy circles on the back of her hand, keeping his eyes fixed on hers. "My pulse never runs out of control when I'm in Madison's presence. Only yours."

Her lips rounded into an oh, and Cameron resisted the urge to capture her lips with his.

She pulled her hand away and Cameron felt its absence like the loss of one of his own limbs.

"Why are you here?" She wrapped her arms around herself.

"The last time I saw you, you had gotten sick all over me and then you told your boss you never wanted to work with me again."

The memory still burned.

"Am I such an ogre that you figured I'd get angry because you were sick?"

"I'm sorry about that. I'll refund you the cost of cleaning or replacing whatever was damaged."

He flung his arms out. "I don't want your money!"

She jumped at his bellow. "Then what do you want?"

"You."

It was true. He wanted to spend time with her without manifesting a reason or cleaning out an old house. She stepped back, angling her chin.

"I'm not sure what you assumed, Mr. Grant, but I'm not that kind of girl."

Her snooty tone amused him. Cameron grinned.

"Do you know how many of those kinds of women I

encounter every day? If I'd wanted one of them, I would have them."

He gentled his voice. "Why'd you run away, Mackenzie? Did you assume I'd be angry?"

"No." She met his gaze and Cameron let out a sigh of relief.

"Then why? Have I given you any reason to believe I'd hold what happened against you?"

After what Vivian had said, he was concerned about how he interacted with his staff. Mackenzie broke eye contact and studied the faded carpet.

"I was ashamed. I'd embarrassed myself in front of you."

"Why did that matter?"

He shifted closer, sensing that whatever she said would rock his world.

She snorted. "Have you seen yourself? I didn't want to be the hostess who'd vomited all over you."

"Would you rather be the woman who made me take my first vacation in a decade?"

"Am I?"

She peered at him. The hint of vulnerability in her eyes made him brave.

"Or how about the woman who has me acting out of character? Maybe you'd like to be the first woman I've been attracted to in years. The only one I want to date."

He gave in to the urge and cupped her face. She leaned into his touch, sending a surge of pleasure rushing through him.

"What happens next?"

She studied his face as she waited for his answer. Cameron allowed himself a few more seconds. Her skin was soft under his palm. Warm. Why had this woman been the one to crawl under his defenses?

Lord, if I'm making a mistake, please make it clear.

Cameron dropped his hand, tucking both of them into his pockets.

"We start by putting this house in some sort of order and maybe," this was harder than he'd expected, "the next time I ask you out, you say yes."

Eleven

Chapter 11

Mackenzie peeked at Cameron. Though it had been hours since his living room confession, she was still processing everything. He had followed her to Orange Valley and then to Cinnamon Hill. Why?

He'd claimed an attraction to her, but there'd been no evidence of it prior to her pretending to be Madison.

That was another thing. How had he been able to tell the difference between the two of them? Their parents and RJ sometimes got confused, not for long, or often, but it still happened.

"Did Madison know you'd figured out that she wasn't me?"

Cameron glanced up from the box he was sorting through, an adorable frown on his face. No, not adorable, just a frown. She was not supposed to admire any part of the man in front of her.

"I don't think so. Why?"

It explained why her sister hadn't called to tell her Cameron Grant had shown up at her house and had guessed their secret.

Maybe she shouldn't admit that part because one thing each of them had on her 'Husband Wishlist' was that the man they married could tell them apart.

No way did she want Madison pushing her to date Cameron, not until she figured out his motives.

"You're attracted to me? You always acted as though I was invisible."

Cameron snorted. "I've never been unaware of you, Mackenzie." His eyes met hers, pinning her in place. "I'm conscious of you the second you enter a room."

"Yeah, right." She rolled her eyes. He must consider her as gullible as a country mouse if he believed she'd fall for that line.

"Shall I prove it to you?" He stood and had moved much too close to her. "Do you remember me asking you that day if you were alright?"

She nodded, her throat too tight to speak.

"Do you know why?"

She shook her head. She needed to get away from this man before she lost control over all her motor functions.

"It was because you weren't acting like yourself. Usually, you sail into a room like you're skating on glass, the tray an inconsequential weight in your hands."

He reached out to touch her face before dropping his hand.

"That day, you didn't. You paused at the door before entering, and then you walked as if the floor was lava. That is until you started speed-walking as though your life depended on it."

"I didn't figure anyone had noticed."

She'd been sure her performance of wellness had been

convincing.

"I always notice you."

Warmth spread through her at the passion that blazed in his eyes.

"I don't know what to make of you. Of us." She shook her head. "I'm not sure if I can conceptualize the idea of us being together."

"We'll ease into it."

He reached for her hand, slipping his fingers between hers. Tingles shot up her arm, as they had the day they'd shook hands. It hadn't been a fluke.

"We've been at this for a while. Why don't we get something to eat?"

Her eyes widened. "In public?"

Hurt flashed in Cameron's eyes. He dropped her hand and stepped back.

"Or not. Maybe I'll talk to you tomorrow."

No, no, no. This was all wrong.

"Wait." She raised a hand toward him, dropping it when he flinched. "I didn't mean it that way. Please don't be upset."

He scoffed. "Explain to me how I should act when the woman I want to date doesn't want to go out in public with me."

His words washed over her, and she grinned.

"I wish I understood why that was funny to you."

His frosty tone was enough to obliterate her grin. Almost.

"You want to date me?"

"Haven't I made that clear?"

Dating Cameron was every childhood and adult fantasy rolled into one. And it would never happen if she couldn't explain to him how she felt.

"But-but..." She stared at the spot beyond his head as she

collected her words.

"You're Cameron Grant. You're practically a celebrity on Saturn Island. And I'm," she lifted a shoulder. "Nobody. People will assume I'm with you because of who you are or what I can get from you."

His eyes darkened. "People will believe what they want. We can't live to curtail public opinion. Besides, you're somebody to me."

She couldn't help it. She grinned. Again. How could she not when this gorgeous man, who could tell her apart from her sister, wanted to date her?

"Enough to turn down your Cameron-ness?"

He lifted a brow. "Is that even a word?"

"It is now. It's like awesomeness, but with you know, you."

A slow smile spread across his face. "From this moment, I'll be incognito Cameron."

"Is that possible?"

For one thing, he stood head and shoulders above most people, including men. For another, his face attracted attention. And would, even if there hadn't been newspaper articles and television programs featuring him.

"You'll see." He reached for her. "Is it okay if I hold your hand?"

"It is." A grin threatened to split her face, the way it would if Cameron had offered her carte blanche to reorganize his house.

"Okay." He took a deep breath and slid his palm against hers. She restrained from swooning. She was going on a date with Cameron Grant. The world had gone topsy-turvy, and she never wanted it to return to being right-side up.

Twelve

Chapter 12

Cameron pulled into the drive-thru of Ham and Burgs as they both agreed they wanted fast food.

"Is this okay?" He stole a glance at her. "That way, we can go back to your place to eat."

Her eyes widened. Cameron coughed.

"I meant the antique shop." He stumbled to get all the words out. "Then we can start working as soon as we're done eating."

What was wrong with him? Had he made a permanent spot in his mouth for his size twelve feet?

"That's fine." She kept her gaze fixed on her hands, which lay folded in her lap.

Lord, I don't know what I'm doing here or why I keep messing up. A little help, please?

He pulled up to the window. Mackenzie put a hand on his thigh. Have mercy.

"Can you get one of those dips for me? Honey mustard,

please."

He plucked her hand off his thigh, holding it as he placed their order.

"Did I do something wrong?"

Cameron crawled to the pickup window, giving the short drive more attention than it deserved.

"When was the last time you went on a date with a guy?"

"I don't date."

He gaped at her. "Ever?"

She shook her head. "Not since high school."

"Don't you want to get married? Have children?"

She cleared her throat. "I want both those things, but…"

Cameron drew in a breath. "But?"

"I've never met a guy that made me want to break my no-dating rule."

What? No wonder she'd been skittish.

"And have you? Do I make you want to break your rule?"

She gave a tiny nod, and Cameron exhaled a sigh of relief. He could do this.

"Don't think I haven't noticed that you haven't answered my question."

"I will." Cameron collected their food and passed everything to her. He drove out of the burger joint, searching for a safe place to stop. He wanted to give her his full attention for this.

"Okay." He turned to face her. "I'm not sure if you're aware of this, but I'm a Christian. My faith is important to me."

Though if he were honest, he'd been less fervent in recent years, but that was going to change. He would take Levi's advice and dig into the Word.

He took one of her hands in his. "I'm extremely attracted to you, Mackenzie, and I want to honor you and God by keeping the physical aspects of our relationship to the bare minimum."

He blew out a breath, took the plunge, and said the words that in some circles would get his man card taken. "I'd appreciate it if we kept all contact above the waist."

She bit her lip and refused to meet his gaze.

"Hey," he tipped her chin up, keeping his hold gentle. "What's wrong?"

"I'm doomed to embarrass myself in front of you." She rolled her eyes. "When I touched you earlier, I didn't think—"

"You don't need to be embarrassed. It was good that we had this talk."

To set his boundaries from early, which was one reason he didn't date. Most women considered him a prude or worse because he didn't want to engage in any premarital "mingling".

* * *

"Why are you doing this by yourself for Christmas?"

Cameron consulted the detailed hand-drawn floor plan Mackenzie had done for the storeroom. The next piece to be moved was an antique armoire. Did everything in this place weigh as much as an old battleship?

Mackenzie glanced at him. "Everyone had something to do. My brother RJ is…somewhere. Mom and Dad are on a cruise and Madison wanted to be out of town for the season."

She rolled her eyes, then went back to entering the latest piece on an inventory list she'd created.

"Besides, it's not as if any of them would have helped, anyway."

There was a lot to unpack in her admission. Where should he start?

"Is your family aware that you're doing this?"

"No."

Guilt and sadness battled for dominance on her face. Cameron went to her, stilling her hands.

"What's going on? Why didn't you tell your family what you'd planned to do?"

Her lips twisted into a sad smile. "And this is where you learn what a pathetic woman you're pursuing."

"Not pathetic." He pulled her over to a loveseat she'd uncovered. "Tell me your story."

"My brother isn't interested in the business. RJ is career-military and had no desire to work with antiques before he joined the army.

"Madison and Dad are all about the restorations. They can't accept that we need to diversify the business for there to be something to pass on to the next generation."

She jerked her shoulder. "Dad never wants to change anything. He believes if it was 'good enough for my grandfather, it's good enough for me.'"

She lowered her voice into what he assumed was an imitation of her father's. He understood the burden she carried.

"Where do you fit in?"

Her eyes blazed with passion. "I love this business. If people became invested in the story behind the pieces, they'd be more likely to buy them and make them part of their own stories. Take this bench we're sitting on," she caressed the intricately carved back.

"The woman who owned this piece sat here when the love of her life proposed to her. Sadly, they never got married because he died before the wedding. But she kept this piece. The reason we have it is that her estate auctioned it after her death."

"How did you learn about their story?"

"Because she told me."

His eyebrows shot up. She grinned. "I'm not crazy, I promise."

She jumped up and dropped to her knees, pushing her hand under the bench. After a bit of wriggling, she waved a leather-bound book in the air.

"Found this one day when I was polishing it. After I read it, I decided not to separate it from the piece."

She accepted his hand and leveraged herself up before plopping down beside him.

"Look at this."

She delicately turned pages until she stopped at a faded photo of a couple seated on the same chair they sat on. Though the photo was poor quality by modern standards, the joy on the couple's faces was evident.

"If I had the money, I'd buy this piece." She closed the journal, resting a hand on it. "Since I don't, I want it to go to a loving home where someone will appreciate it. Not shoved into oblivion in an antique store or buried under a pile of junk."

He understood. This project was about validation. Mackenzie wanted to prove her worth to her family by giving them something they hadn't yet realized they needed. Something he empathized with all too well.

"Enough about me. What about you? Why aren't you spending Christmas with your family?"

"What family? The father who marries and divorces women like it's an Olympic sport? Or the mother who doesn't understand she needs to be an active part in her adult son's life?"

"But you guys always seem so close in the pictures..." She

bit her lip as she trailed off.

"A picture tells a thousand stories, not all of them true." He pinched the bridge of his nose. "The only time my mother acknowledges my existence is when she's trying to marry me off to the daughter of someone she wants to impress."

Cameron pressed his lips together at the horror on Mackenzie's face. He took calming breaths and waited until the anger and disillusionment at his family had returned to their usual simmer.

God, when will I stop being angry at my parents?

"Money doesn't eradicate the problems in people's lives, Mackenzie. Most times, it amplifies them."

Thirteen

Chapter 13

Sympathy welled up in her heart for him. He kept up a decent facade, but he was hurting. How dare his family not recognize what a wonderful man their son was?

"You know what?" Mackenzie put the journal on the seat beside them. "We don't need them." She jumped off the bench, tugging him to his feet. "We'll be each other's family."

Cameron stared down at her. This close, she had to crane her neck to meet his gaze. Their height difference should have intimidated her, instead, she felt safe.

"I don't want you in my family, Mackenzie, not unless you're applying to fill a specific role."

Oh my. The passion in his eyes left no mistake about what role he wanted her to play. Her mouth went dry. How was she supposed to get out of this conversational corner she'd talked herself into?

She propped a hand on her hip and channeled all the

sassiness she could muster.

"That's step thirteen, Mr. Grant. We must get through the other twelve steps first."

Cameron chuckled. "Alright, Mackenzie. Since I'm counting on us to make it all the way to step thirteen. Let's get those twelve steps out of the way."

Mackenzie's mind short-circuited. Was Cameron hinting that he hoped their relationship would end in marriage? The idea stole her breath.

Lord, I'm out of my depth here. Cameron wants to marry me. What am I supposed to do?

Show him what family means.

"Mackenzie?" Cameron touched the back of her hand. "Are you alright? What just happened?"

She half-smiled as she blinked up at him. "You won't believe me if I tell you."

"Try me."

"God wants me to show you what family is."

An emotion she couldn't decipher filled Cameron's eyes, turning the light gray stormy. His Adam's apple bobbed as he swallowed. "Okay, we just started dating and set all those boundaries in place, but I could use a hug."

"Sure."

Cameron wrapped his arms around her, cradling her as if she was the most precious gift. Her heart sighed as she nestled close to him. He truly smelled like sunshine—leathery with a hint of citrus.

"Thank you." Cameron pressed a kiss to her forehead.

She wasn't sure why God wanted her to get close to this man, but she'd obey. Even though he had the power to break down all her defenses.

Chapter 13

Please, God, don't let Cameron break my heart.

** * **

Mackenzie pointed to a parking lot that was already half-full.

"Park there." When he had, she turned to him. "Where's the incognito Cameron you promised me?"

Cameron held up a finger before reaching into the dashboard for a ball cap and a pair of shades.

She smirked at him. "That's your disguise?"

"Hey, it worked for Clark Kent."

He put them on and grinned. "Don't I look different?"

She scowled at him. Because he did. It must be a guy thing. Her glasses had done nothing to protect her identity from him.

"In another half an hour, you won't need those shades when the sun sets."

"I'll still keep them on." He waggled his eyebrows. "Pretend I'm a celebrity. Wait there."

Cameron jumped out of the car, hurrying around to her side. She suppressed a grin when he opened the door for her.

"You know I can open the door for myself, right?"

"Yes." He took one of her hands in his. "But it gives me a chance to do this." He slipped his fingers between hers. "Where are we going?"

"You'll see. Are you hungry?"

"I could eat."

As if on cue, his stomach rumbled. Mackenzie laughed.

"Food is never far from your thoughts, is it?"

"Hey, it takes a lot to keep this bear in motion."

"Whatever. I need to stop by the pharmacy first."

"Sure." Cameron changed direction at her tug without

another word.

Mackenzie smiled at the cashier. "Two tickets, please."

She reached into her pocket for money, but Cameron was there in an instant, wallet open. "The gentleman always pays."

Warmth suffused her entire body. She wasn't a damsel in distress, but Cameron made her feel feminine and special. What would it be like to let him care for her?

"What's this?" Cameron angled the sheet of paper that came with their ticket toward her.

"This, Sir Incognito, is how Cinnamon Hill does dinner and a movie at Christmas."

"This is a shopping list. Or a treasure hunt."

Mackenzie laughed at his puzzled expression, pulling him out of the way of the customer behind them.

"It's more of a treasure hunt—the best kind. Every year, businesses come together for this event. Each provides one meal or experience, which all blends together into the perfect evening."

She pointed at the first group of names on the list. "Everyone in this group has agreed to provide appetizers, and this is the list of what each stop provides."

Cameron stroked his chin. "So, I can eat as much as I want because I bought a ticket?"

She jostled him. "No. You get a serving size." She leaned closer. "Though some vendors are more generous than others."

"Aren't they afraid someone will take advantage of them? Anyone can go up to them and claim they're taking part in this dinner and a movie thing."

"There's an honor system and a limit for each category. Besides, people have to show their tickets in order to get served without paying at each of the stops."

"Alright."

At his disgruntled tone, Mackenzie laid a hand on his arm. "No one is getting ripped off in this, Cam. The vendors get extra foot traffic and the community gets a fun event they can enjoy. It's a win-win. Don't you trust anyone?"

"No. People are always seeking to get more than they give."

This poor man. Pity rushed through Mackenzie for him. How sad to go through life, always expecting people to take advantage of him.

It made him showing up here looking for her much more significant. Despite how jaded he'd become about human nature, he'd put himself out of his comfort zone. For her.

This was why God wanted her to show Cameron what it meant to have a family. To remind him there were still people on earth who cared about him, wanting nothing in return.

Earlier, she'd worried that Cameron had the power to break her heart. Now she worried about the impact she'd have on him.

Please, God, don't let me hurt him.

Fourteen

Chapter 14

Cameron shook off the gloom that had overtaken him in the pharmacy. The pity in Mackenzie's eyes had hit him in the gut.

It wasn't that he hadn't met wonderful people. He had. But talking about his parents earlier had been a painful reminder that he was alone for Christmas. Usually, he planned it so he had deadlines to accomplish over the holidays, or spent them far away from home.

Loneliness was something he'd gotten used to a long time ago. He glanced down at Mackenzie. She'd tucked her arm into his and let him lead her out of the pharmacy. She hadn't said a word, though it was clear he had no clue what he was doing. Or where he needed to go first.

Why was he drawn to this woman? Her words flashed through his mind.

God wants me to show you what family is.

Was this God's way of reminding him that though his earthly parents left a lot to be desired, his Heavenly Father was watching out for him?

Even if my father and mother abandon me, the LORD will hold me close.

Shame rushed through him. He'd been so focused on the pain of his family situation that he was overlooking the gift of this present moment. Mackenzie was also alone for the holidays, but she wasn't whining about it.

Instead, she was squirreling him around in the cold when she probably wanted to be inside where it was warm.

"I'm sorry." He stopped in the middle of the sidewalk, forcing people to move around them. "I'm not used to giving people the benefit of the doubt."

The thought of businesses giving people their products on an honor system was enough to make him shudder.

"It's okay." Mackenzie's eyes twinkled with mischief. "I figured it wasn't your time of the year."

"Come again?"

"Don't bears hibernate for winter?"

"Ha-ha." He allowed his lips to curve into a smile. "Where do we go first?"

"I always get the jerked chicken wings and the fried plantains." She shrugged. "The soup would be good since it's cold today. But I'll defer to you since you're the newbie. What do you want?"

He studied the paper. "I'll have what you're having."

"No. If you order the same thing I do, how will we mix and match?"

He chuckled. "Okay. Banana fritters?" He peeked at her to judge her response. She nodded. "And...?"

"Plantains."

"Weren't you having those?"

"You can't have three appetizers, silly."

"I can buy you a cup of soup, Mackenzie."

She angled her chin. "I can buy myself a cup of soup, Mr. Grant. But that defeats the point of the event."

"Alright." He faked a long-suffering sigh. "Guess I'm having the plantains."

She beamed at him and Cameron suspected he'd do a lot of things for her if it would make her look at him like that—as if he was her hero and had fought a dragon for her.

* * *

Cameron took in the rows of blue tents that had been erected in the middle of the street.

"They closed the roads?"

"Just this street and only for the week."

"What do we do next?" He pitched his voice to be heard over the Christmas carols that boomed from speakers on the sidewalk.

"We find the vendors that have what we want and get our eating on."

She did a little shoulder shimmy that jostled his arm. He grinned down at her.

"Let's do it."

Being with Mackenzie made him feel more alive than he had in years. Why? Most people assumed he had the best life imaginable. He had more money than he could spend in a lifetime, a business he enjoyed, and the opportunity to travel the world. If he wanted to.

Yet here he was, in disguise, traipsing all over town because a woman made him want to try things he'd never considered before.

"Mackenzie—"

"Madison! Girl, I have been calling your name for the last five minutes." A medium-built woman in an ugly Christmas sweater rushed up to them, two small children in tow.

Mackenzie met his gaze and mouthed, 'Sorry'.

"Hi, Shelby. How are you?" Mackenzie smiled at the woman.

"Girl, you know how it is. Running around with these kids takes up all my time. When you have a few of your own, you'll understand."

Mackenzie's smile tightened. Cameron studied her. What was that about? Did not being a mother bother her?

"You can't have children without a husband."

Mackenzie's upbeat tone was so full of false cheer that it was a wonder Shelby didn't catch it.

"I hear you." Shelby leaned in with a conspiratorial wink. "I see you're working on that part. Who's your friend?"

Shelby gave him a coquettish look, and he struggled not to roll his eyes.

"Oh, this is…"

"CJ." Cameron chimed in before Mackenzie blew their cover. "Nice to meet you." He tipped his chin in her direction.

"And you." Shelby wiggled her fingers at him, ignoring the children who'd begun twisting the ends of her sweater.

"Mummy, I need to go." One of them whined. Shelby forced a laugh.

"Talk to you later. Motherhood calls."

They remained in place as Shelby rushed off, lifting the smaller child as they fast-walked to what must be the nearest restroom.

"CJ?" Mackenzie arched a brow at him.

"My middle name is James. My father wanted me to be a Junior, but my mother outranked him. Gave me his name as a middle name instead."

She scanned him from head to toe. "Not as catchy as Incognito Cameron, but it will do."

"Why did the conversation with Shelby bother you?"

She peered at him in surprise.

"I notice you, Mackenzie."

"She helped me understand why Madison didn't wish to be here for the holidays."

Cameron empathized. The holidays were hard for those who didn't have a traditional family.

Fifteen

Chapter 15

Shelby had put a damper on Mackenzie's mood. Was this what Madison had to go through? The constant reminder that she didn't have children? Or that she wouldn't?

It must wear on her sister, whose PCOS diagnosis meant motherhood was almost impossible for her. She shook off her morbid thoughts. This wasn't the time or place to moan over sad things. She had a mission to accomplish.

"Are you ready for the next course?" She plastered a smile on her face for Cameron.

"Are you going to tell me what's going on?"

"It's not my story to tell." She cast her gaze over to the couple who sat at the table with them. They were college-aged and so wrapped up in each other that they'd neglected their food.

Still, it wouldn't do to share Madison's story. It wasn't hers to tell.

He sighed and stood, holding a hand out for her. "Let's go to the next stop."

As they veered away from what Mackenzie had dubbed "Appetizer Aisle", she tried to remember the list of restaurants on this year's flyer. She stopped under the next streetlight.

"Where are we going?"

Cameron peered down at her, his shades long since discarded as she'd predicted. "That's what I'd like to know."

"What do you mean?"

Something told her they were no longer talking about a restaurant.

"Mackenzie, I like you, and I get that this is all new for you, but it's new for me, too. I have never felt this way about a woman. This thing between us won't work if we're reluctant to be open with each other.

"I've shared things with you I've never disclosed to anyone else. But you," he took a deep breath before continuing, "you've compartmentalized your life and only share the surface layer with me."

He was right. She wasn't used to sharing her thoughts and emotions with anyone but Madison. Except...

The burden she carried because her sister couldn't have children wasn't one she could discuss with her twin. They'd read that the children of identical twins were both cousins and half-siblings. They'd planned to have children as close together as possible and raise them as siblings.

"You're hurting. How can I fix it if you won't tell me what's wrong?"

Oh. Her heart plopped out of her chest and fell at his feet.

"Madison can't have children. It's why she didn't want to be here for the holidays. I don't blame her. Not when she has to deal with people like that." She flung her arm in the direction they'd come from.

She was fired up now. "Why is having children the badge of motherhood? Who determined that when a woman can't have a child, through no fault of her own, that she's somehow less than?"

Her eyes filled with tears. It wasn't fair.

"Oh, princess." Cameron folded her into his arms.

"We were supposed to become moms at the same time. Raise our children together as half-siblings."

"You can still do that. There's no reason you can't be a surrogate for your sister. Or offer her one of your eggs. There are many ways to become a mother these days."

She scoffed. "What man would want his wife to carry another man's child? Or would give away his wife's child to be raised by another family?"

"I would."

She pulled away to look at him. "Yeah, right."

"If it was important to you or would make you happy, I'd do it."

His sincerity shone in his eyes. Was it possible to fall in love in such a short time? If it was, she'd fallen in love with Cameron.

She was supposed to be showing him what it meant to be part of a family, yet he'd already shown her more about that than she'd experienced in twenty-six years of living.

* * *

Cameron stopped at the hostess stand and glanced around. "Are you sure I'm not underdressed for this place?"

Mackenzie smirked up at him. "Not tonight."

Usually, The Flamingo was one of the most upscale restaurants in Cinnamon Hill. A single meal cost more than her week's salary. If you weren't wearing your best, you wouldn't make it past the threshold because of their strict dress code.

"They break the rules for Christmas Week."

Cameron frowned at her. "What does that even mean?"

"You'll find out soon." Mackenzie smiled at the hostess, who'd been following their conversation like her own personal reality show. "Hi, Becky. Can we have a table for two? Somewhere secluded, please."

"Sure." Becky winked at them. "First date? I got you, Madison. Follow me."

Mackenzie's cheeks burned. Whether it was from being mistaken for her sister or because Becky had assumed she was on a date with Cameron, she wasn't sure.

Either way, she'd have to tell Emmy what was going on. Before someone called to ask about her mysterious date.

Cameron pulled out the seat for her and waited until Becky left. He leaned across the table to whisper.

"Did we pass a family wearing plaid pajamas?"

Mackenzie grinned. "The Howards. They own the department store. I believe they use Christmas Week as a marketing tactic. Last year, everyone was in suits. Even the girls. And somehow, by next week, whatever they showed up in here will either be out of stock or low on supply."

"Hmm. Maybe your family should do something similar."

She arched a brow. "Wear costumes?"

"No. As beautiful as you'd look dressed retro, that's not what I mean. Maybe you can loan out antique pieces for the week. It may generate some interest in what your family sells."

Chapter 15

Why hadn't that occurred to her before?

"That's brilliant." She beamed at him, not caring if the whole of Cinnamon Hill was there to witness it.

"I get the occasional idea to go with my bear strength."

"Hmm."

Suddenly, all she could think about was the way he'd held and comforted her. Mackenzie had never met a man who made her want to play the damsel in distress. Until Cameron. She'd play lady to his knight any day of the week.

Time was slipping away. Soon, Cameron's two-week vacation would be up and he'd return to his normal life. Without her. Leaving her to pick up the pieces of her broken heart.

Sixteen

Chapter 16

The second Mackenzie answered the phone, Cameron started his spiel.

"What are you doing Sunday afternoon at three?"

She laughed, the sound lifting his spirits until the corner of his mouth curved in response.

"That's an oddly specific question. Why do you ask?"

"Because I have an oddly specific plan."

He'd grown up not having to worry about money. He'd taken his family's successful business and turned it into an empire. Cameron made his first billion by the time he was twenty-five.

He'd always assumed that when he met a woman he wanted to pursue, he'd treat them to the lavish lifestyle they deserved.

"Well? Are you free?"

He smiled ruefully as he waited for Mackenzie's response. He'd found the woman he wanted to date, but she didn't want him to spend money on her. Mackenzie wouldn't allow him to buy her a cup of soup.

It made it more challenging for him to come up with date ideas that were also inexpensive. And wouldn't reveal his identity. Was being with Mackenzie worth it?

Who can find a virtuous and capable wife? She is more precious than rubies.

"I might be. For the right person."

Cameron pictured her teasing smile. The way her eyes lit up when she smiled at him. Yes. She was worth it.

"I'll pick you up at two. Dress casually. And wear warm clothes."

"I didn't say I was going out with you."

"You said you were available for the right person. I'm the right man, Mackenzie. For you."

Sunday afternoon wouldn't come soon enough. After realizing the amount of work that needed to be done in his uncle's house, he agreed with Mackenzie's assessment. The place needed professional cleaners.

Vivian had hired a firm. They had sent a team that had spent the past three days cleaning the house, both interior and exterior.

Since Mackenzie had claimed she didn't need his help at the store, he'd had too much time on his hands. He'd kept his promise to himself and his friend and had spent hours in the Word, poring over the book of Proverbs.

To say he'd spent a lot of time in Proverbs 31 would be a gross understatement. He'd studied the chapter, praying, reading commentaries, and taking copious notes.

Was Mackenzie a Proverbs 31 woman? His gut told him yes. Was that why he was drawn to her? Why he sensed God encouraging him to spend time with her?

* * *

Cameron pulled up in front of a two-story blue and white house. The front yard was lush with vegetation that reminded him of Mackenzie's house in Orange Valley.

Green tinsel wrapped around the banister and up the column. Strings of lights nestled among the foliage. Had Mackenzie decorated? Or had her parents done it before they'd left on vacation?

A large wreath hung on the front door, which swung open before he knocked. His gaze swept over Mackenzie, who wore blue jeans and a rose-pink sweater that invited his touch. She'd pulled her hair into a high ponytail that gave her a youthful appearance.

She was the girl next door again. He groaned.

"What?" She lifted a hand to brush over her hair. "Do I look okay?"

"Perfect."

"Then why did you groan? Are you in pain? Did you hurt yourself?"

She rested the back of her hand against his forehead and would have patted him down if he hadn't grabbed her hand.

"I'm fine." He almost growled the words. "I prefer you as the polished hostess. This thing you have going that's a cross between the girl next door and the sexy librarian is driving me crazy."

A slow smile spread across her face. "Is that so?"

"Yes." He tugged her toward him. "Let's get to where we're going fast. We need to be around lots of people. You're wreaking havoc on my self-control."

As soon as they'd settled in the car, she turned to him.

"Where's this oddly specific place you're taking me?"

"To a basketball game."

Her brow furrowed and regret crashed over him. He hadn't asked if she enjoyed the sport. He'd made plans and expected her to fall in line. He was a boar.

"I'm sorry. I should have asked if you were okay with attending a match. We can do something else."

His brain began tossing out alternative ideas. Canceling the date was not an option. He didn't want to give her the chance to comprehend what a fool he was and slam the door to her heart that had cracked open the tiniest bit.

She touched the back of his hand. "You enjoy basketball?"

He nodded.

"Why?"

His eyes flicked to where her hand rested on his, then back to her eyes. No one had ever asked him that before. Maybe because no one had ever cared enough to find out what he did when he wasn't working.

"I played basketball in high school. Some of my best memories are on the court or related to a basketball game."

"And the team that's playing today?"

"One of the best—led by my high school coach. This isn't an official game as it's a fundraiser for charity."

He followed Coach Peters' matches like they were pro basketball. His mentor had been more of a father than the man whose DNA ran through him.

"Then we should go."

She released his hand to buckle her seatbelt. He already missed the warmth of her touch.

"I want to know what's important to you, and to support you when you do them."

His heart swelled at her words. What had he done to deserve this woman?

"What step are we on now?"

Her eyebrows flew up. "Excuse me?"

"You said marriage was the thirteenth step—that there were twelve steps to get through first. What step are we on now? And what step do we need to be at before I get to kiss you?"

She gave a breathy laugh. "Wouldn't you love to find out?"

"Yes."

Her tinkle of laughter surrounded him in the small space.

"I'll write them down for you."

"Please do." He started the engine. "While you're at it, tell me if there are any cheat codes. I want to fast-forward to that kiss."

Seventeen

Chapter 17

S itting in front-row seats at a stadium watching a college basketball match was not how she'd expected to be spending a Sunday afternoon. Especially not with Cameron, once again decked in his incognito garb.

Cameron wanted to kiss her. What would that be like? She stole a glance at him, cheeks burning when she caught him staring at her.

"What?"

He leaned closer to her and pressed his lips against her ear. "The crowd's not helping. I still want to kiss you."

She fanned her heated cheeks. "Maybe if you kept your eyes on the game, CJ."

"Hmm. Maybe." He murmured, making no attempt to shift his gaze.

"Okay, Sir Incognito." She tapped the brow of his cap. "Which team am I cheering for and which one should I boo?"

He grinned before glancing at the teams on the court. Whew! Too much of Cameron's concentrated attention was dangerous. She took measured breaths until her pulse evened out.

"So we're the blue team?" After his confirmation, she watched the game with interest. The two teams were evenly matched and at the end of the first half, they both had the same score on the board.

"They'd do a lot better if Number 12 would tilt his feet before attempting to shoot. Then his shoulders wouldn't keep locking up and maybe he could sink the ball." She folded her arms and leaned back against the bench with a huff.

Cameron looked at her, amazement stamped on his features. "You're a fan?"

She jerked a shoulder. "My brother fancied himself the next Michael Jordan for a while."

RJ had used his free time to convince either her or Madison to play him one-on-one. Sometimes both of them at once.

"Huh. Every time I find out something new about you, I'm more intrigued."

The way he was studying her made her want to tell him all her secrets. She would make some up if he kept looking at her that way—as if she were a precious jewel he'd been searching for and had finally found.

"I'm going to use the restroom." She'd join the line even if it extended into the town square to have a few moments of privacy to get herself back under control.

Things were moving way too fast. How was it she had this depth of emotion for him already?

Technically, she'd known Cameron Grant for two years, but that had been different. He'd been her client and nothing else. Sure, in the privacy of her own thoughts, she'd admired him and the way he never pressed himself on any of the servers—unlike some other crafts she'd worked on. There were some clients with whom she never took a nap unless she had locked and bolted the crew door. Even then, she wore several layers of clothing. Just in case.

Was it wrong to crave something more than a temporary connection between her and Cameron? To forget they lived in two different worlds? To believe he wanted the same happily ever after for them as she did? Maybe.

Better to enjoy their flirtation without allowing herself to believe he wanted to marry her. She wouldn't get hurt that way.

"You won't get to leave."

Her eyes swung to his face. His eyes sparkled with mischief. She frowned at him. "Why?"

He pointed. Mackenzie swiveled her head. Her face and Cameron's were super-sized on the screen before them, in a frame of mistletoe. The words Mistletoe Kiss Cam were in fat, red letters above their heads. She glared at him.

"Did you have something to do with this?"

His eyes danced. "Me? This is one of those cases where God is granting me the desires of my heart."

She huffed out a laugh. "You're crazy. Well, I'm not following instructions from an inanimate object."

"Kiss. Kiss. Kiss." The chant started behind her. Mackenzie glared at the white-haired man who eavesdropped on their conversation.

"Don't you have anything better to do than watch two strangers kiss?"

"No, ma'am. Not today." The man grinned and resumed his chant, elbowing the man next to him until he started chanting as well.

"It doesn't matter." She folded her arms across her chest. "If we don't play along, they'll move on to someone else."

Cameron crumpled his face in an admirable imitation of a sulky toddler. "But I wanna play, Kenzie."

She snorted out a laugh. "Behave."

In a matter of minutes, the entire auditorium was chanting. "Kiss. Kiss. Kiss."

Mackenzie rolled her eyes and turned to Cameron. "Can you believe this?"

"Nope." Cameron balled his hands into fists, beating them against his thighs in tandem with the chant. "Kiss me. Kiss me. Kiss me."

She snickered at his modified chant. "Alright, you big baby." She leaned over to brush her lips against his cheek.

The crowd groaned in disappointment. She glanced up at the floating camera. Another couple must have replaced them. But no, it was still on her and Cameron.

"Oh, come on." She threw up a hand. "I kissed him."

Words began scrolling across the bottom of the screen.

Cameron read them aloud. "You call that a kiss? You can do better than that."

She slapped a hand over her face. No doubt this story will make the rounds through Cinnamon Hill by tomorrow.

If she had kissed him instead of making such a big deal about it, the camera would have moved on and everyone would have been talking about something else.

Instead, by refusing, she'd brought attention to them. She groaned. Why did life have so many tough choices?

"Hey," Cameron turned her face to his, using one of his hands to shield them from the camera. "You don't have to do this. We can leave." He tugged on her with the other hand and would have stood if she hadn't exerted all her effort into resisting him.

"Wait." This basketball match was something he wanted to do. From the way Cameron had talked about his old coach, she understood that being here was important to him. "I'll do it. It's a simple kiss."

He searched her gaze. "Are you sure?"

No, she wasn't sure of anything. Mackenzie nodded. This wasn't her first kiss but after her dating disasters in high school…

"Let's just do it."

"If you're sure."

"I am." Mackenzie leaned toward Cameron, expecting him to do the same. Instead, he lifted a hand to her cheek, caressing it as though it were the smoothest satin. The most expensive cashmere.

"Mackenzie."

He leaned in, his lips brushing against hers in a feather-soft touch. She'd been mistaken. This wasn't a simple kiss. Though his lips barely touched hers, it was as if an explosion happened behind her eyes. In her pulse. Throughout her whole body.

If this was a simple kiss, then Cameron had ruined her lips for everyone except him.

She pulled back, pleased that his eyes held the same shock that resonated through her. What on earth had just happened? And what were they supposed to do about it?

Eighteen

Chapter 18

Mackenzie Porter had ruined him for other women. Because she'd lied. That wasn't a simple kiss. That had been a rocket launch. An explosion. The end of life as he'd known it.

Cameron had kissed other women before, but never had he wanted to drag the woman to the nearest altar to make their relationship official.

Why had the stupid camera moved on? Why couldn't it remain on them all evening so he could have more mind-blowing kisses with Mackenzie?

The match resumed on the court and though his eyes were on the players, he was unaware of them. What he was conscious of was Mackenzie. The light, flowery scent wafting up from her skin. The way she'd gone still and had been careful not to touch him since they'd broken the kiss. Had he lost her?

His mind raced as he considered what he'd do if she refused

to see him again. That was not an option. Being with Mackenzie had become as essential as air. The trouble was, how would he convince her of this truth?

Cameron turned to Mackenzie at the final buzzer. "We won."

Around them, the fans' exhilaration filled the air. The cheers and shouts should have been ear-splitting. Yet, it was as if he and Mackenzie were in an eerie bubble. One where everything faded into the distance.

"Congratulations." Her lips curved into a smile and he almost gave in to the urge to kiss her again. Instead, he brushed his knuckles over the back of her hand.

"Are we okay?"

"Of course."

He searched her eyes to decipher the truth of her feelings. Had he read her wrong? Had she shrunk back after the kiss, or had he been projecting? Was he the one who'd pulled away?

"Mac—"

"Someone's trying to get your attention." She tipped her chin toward the court.

Cameron peeked over his shoulder, standing as the older man approached. His coach had the same wiry build he'd had when Cameron was in high school. The only difference was that he'd gone bald at the top, while the hair around the fringes had grayed.

"Coach Peters." Cameron gave his mentor a man-hug, affection for him, pushing away his annoyance at the interruption.

"Who do we have here?"

Coach Peters beamed at Mackenzie. Cameron held out a hand for her. She stared at it before slipping her hand into his.

"This is Mackenzie." Cameron kept his fingers tangled with hers. Coach Peters grinned at their joined hands.

"Good to see you here with a lady friend." The coach winked at Mackenzie. "I've been encouraging him to date for the last five years. Ever since Sylvia—"

"Coach." He infused a note of warning into his tone. Not that Coach Peters was afraid of him, but maybe he'd take pity on him. Cameron felt Mackenzie's curious gaze on him and suppressed a sigh. Ready or not, he would have to talk about Sylvia.

* * *

Cameron walked Mackenzie to her front door. She had spent several minutes talking to Coach Peters and had even spoken to the team, commending them on their performance. She'd remained silent on the drive home. Unnaturally quiet.

"Who's Sylvia?"

As much as he hated talking about Sylvia, he'd rather have Mackenzie sharing her thoughts than push them inward. He gestured to the lounge chair.

"Can we sit?"

She sank into the seat, her eyes clinging to his face. He sat beside her before popping back up.

"Sylvia's one of my father's ex-wives."

Did that make her his stepmother? Or ex-stepmother, to be exact. Best not to dwell on that. He focused on Mackenzie's face. The confusion and openness made his knees buckle.

Usually, when he told this story, he was the one who got the blame—as if he'd set out to seduce his father's wife. He dropped onto the seat beside her, relief making his shoulders sag, especially when she shifted a little closer to him.

"I met Sylvia at a real estate conference in Port Martin. I

attend those once in a while to keep up with what's going on in the industry. She was a couple of years older than me, but we hit it off immediately."

She'd claimed to be a realtor, though he'd found out later that her only talent was acting.

"We started dating. Within two weeks, she was pressing for more intimacy. I explained my beliefs and though she claimed she understood, she didn't stop." He shook his head, angry at how gullible he'd been.

"She wanted me to marry her. I refused. Less than a week later, she showed up at a company event on my father's arm. Three weeks later, they were married."

Her eyes widened. He scoffed. "Yeah. Turns out she and my father had been dating. After he dumped her, she planned her revenge. She created a persona for herself and set out to deceive me."

Would Sylvia have married him if he'd given in to the pressure and proposed?

"I'm sorry." She rested a hand on his arm. "Did you love her?"

Had he? Her pursuit of him had flattered him. At first. It had soon become tiring.

"No."

"It bothered you?"

"Of course. She pretended to be someone she wasn't."

She grimaced. "The way I did when I switched places with Madison." She withdrew her hand. "I'm sorry."

"No." He reached for her, clasping her hand. Her hand was much smaller than his. "It's not the same as what Sylvia did. It was all a game to her."

And to his father, who'd been smug that Cameron had dated a woman he'd broken up with. For James, it had been a badge of honor that his girlfriend, and then wife, was young enough to appeal to Cameron.

James Grant had been quick to reconcile with Sylvia after the woman had claimed she'd been out of her mind with grief. Their marriage had lasted less than eighteen months. Cameron suspected Sylvia's pain had been over the money in his father's bank account rather than the man himself.

"It's not your fault." Mackenzie clutched his hand. How could there be such strength in the slender fingers?

"Wasn't it? I was the one who didn't realize the woman was playing me."

"Are you responsible for her motives as well?" Mackenzie's eyes bore into his. "She was a greedy woman who targeted you as part of her scheme. You did nothing wrong. You were a victim."

Her words washed over him like a soothing balm, healing wounds he'd believed had scabbed over. Anger and hurt that he'd held onto for years fell away.

"Thank you." He pressed a kiss to her palm. Gratitude for this woman who already meant so much to him filled his heart.

Please, God, don't let me mess this up.

Nineteen

Chapter 19

"Where do we go from here?" Mackenzie said the first thing that popped into her head. Anything to take her mind off the sensations that swirled through her at the press of Cameron's lips on her skin.

The peace on his face made it clear he was no longer worried about his past or the treacherous woman who'd deceived him.

Didn't women understand that when one of them acted poorly, it cast a shadow on every woman? It was the reason some men struggled to trust the women in their lives. Because someone had deceived or betrayed them.

"I have no clue."

Mackenzie smirked at him. "Your grand plan was to take me to a basketball game? Suppose I'd hated it?"

"No." He touched the tip of her nose. "I'd planned to take you out for dinner. To find a fast food place where we'd pretend to be teenagers again and load up on more calories than we should."

She had to admit, that would have been fun.

"And now?"

He twirled the end of her ponytail around his finger. "I don't want to move. I fear that we'll go somewhere and someone will intrude on our peace and you'll pull back. The way you did today. After our kiss?" His eyes searched hers. "Did I imagine it?"

She shook her head.

"Why?"

She inhaled a shaky breath. How much should she tell him? The betrayal he'd experienced at Sylvia's hand loosened her tongue.

"No one has ever kissed me like that before. The emotions…" Her cheeks burned, and she dropped her gaze. He must consider her a fool. An unsophisticated twit.

His fingers brushed her ear. "Me neither."

Shock—at the sensation and his words—had her eyes flying up to meet his.

"You mean?" Her tongue darted out to moisten her lips. His eyes traced the path.

"Don't do that. The Kiss Cam pushed us along a few steps, but we're not there yet. Kissing you today made me want more, and we're not ready."

His honesty made her want to learn everything about him. To skip a few more steps on their non-existent timeline.

"So," she drew the word into three syllables. "What should we do instead?"

"You'll go inside to get blankets." He held up his phone. "I'll order food."

"Why don't we go inside?" She gestured to the house behind

her.

His gaze snapped to her lips and back. "Hmm. No."

Why did she keep doing that? Mackenzie jumped up. She was no better than Sylvia. She moved blindly toward the house.

"Mackenzie."

"I'll—"

In less than a second, he'd covered the distance between them.

"Hey." He cradled her face in his hands. "We'll figure this out together." He pressed a kiss to her forehead.

Don't hurt him.

"Okay." She clung to him for a second. She hoped they'd figure it out soon because she wanted more. More time with him. More dates. She wouldn't be content until she knew him as well as she did herself.

In less than half an hour, they'd built a fort using blankets and her mother's veranda chairs. Ten minutes later, their food arrived.

They ate and talked about everything from high school to favorite movies to childhood memories. At some point, she snuggled against him, her head brushing against his shoulder.

The hours slipped away until sleep announced its presence by tugging on her eyelids. After her third yawn in as many seconds, Cameron sat up.

"I should go."

"No."

He touched the tip of her nose. "You're half asleep. Don't worry. I'll be back."

She disentangled herself from him with reluctance and allowed him to pull her to her feet.

He tucked a blanket around her and escorted her to the front door.

"One second." He hurried back to grab the pile of blankets. "Where do you want them?"

She stepped back and pointed to the couch, struggling to keep her eyes open. He was back in a second.

"Close the door behind me." He brushed his knuckles over her cheek. "Sleep tight, MyKenzie."

* * *

"Why am I on the evening news kissing a guy on the Mistletoe Cam? And why is everybody in Cinnamon Hill calling to ask me about my mystery man? Who is the mystery man?"

Mackenzie groaned as her sister's words assaulted her ears. "What time is it?"

"Are you still sleeping?"

Mackenzie flipped the phone to check the time, bolting up in bed when she did. 9:30. How had she slept through her alarm?

Memories of the previous evening flooded her mind, and a slow smile crept over her face. One she was glad her sister couldn't see because there would be even more questions to answer.

"Can't talk, Emmy. I have to go. I'm late."

Her phone notification beeped. Madison wanted to switch to a video call.

No. No. No. No. No!

She swiped the video icon before it was too late. Her sister's concerned face pressed close to the screen.

"Are you okay?"

"Of course." She tried an innocent look. Hard to do when the other person knows your face and all your expressions intimately. "I'm fine."

"Did you forget what day it is?"

"Uhm…"

"It's the twenty-third." Madison supplied. "The day of the auction. Did you forget?"

It may have slipped her mind with so many other delicious things to think about.

"What time is it again?"

"2:30."

Since the office would be closed for the rest of the year, Mackenzie relaxed. She could get a few more hours of sleep and then get up in time to have a leisurely breakfast before the auction.

Maybe she'd invite Cameron to accompany her. A smile crept over her face.

"What is going on with you?" Madison arched a brow. "You're glowing."

"I am not!" She was. Her cheeks hurt from the pressure of suppressing her smile.

"I'm still waiting for you to answer me. Who were you kissing at the basketball game?"

Madison's words penetrated her Cameron fog.

"Who told you about that?"

Madison smirked at her. "It made the news."

Must have been a slow news day. Or another side effect of her making a bigger deal about the Mistletoe Kiss Cam than had been necessary.

"Emmy, I wanna go to the park. You said we'd go if I ate my breakfast."

A soft smile crept across Madison's face at the childish voice.

"Whose child is that?" Mackenzie squinted at the screen.

"And where are you?"

When Mackenzie had answered the call, she'd focused on fending off Madison's questions. Now she studied the background. Madison was in a kitchen, but not hers. Her kitchen walls were yellow, not blue.

"Did you paint my kitchen?"

Madison whipped her head around. "What? No! Why would I do that?"

Mackenzie pointed at the wall beyond Madison's shoulder. "Then why is my kitchen the wrong color? Who is the child in the background? Where are you?"

Guilt flooded Madison's features before it disappeared. "I have to go."

Before Mackenzie said another word, the call disconnected. Mackenzie redialed her sister's number, not surprised when Madison refused the call.

It's a good thing the antique shop was closed for the rest of the holidays because her sister was keeping secrets. The trepidation that skittered down Mackenzie's spine told her it was a big one.

Lord, I don't know what's going on with Madison, but You do. Please keep her safe.

She'd attend the auction and then, as hard as it would be to tear herself away from Cameron, she'd return to Orange Valley to check on Madison.

Twenty

Chapter 20

Cameron woke with a smile on his face. His first thought was of Mackenzie. Was she awake yet? Was it too soon to call her?

They'd had an amazing night and considering that they hadn't done more than cuddle under blankets, talk, and eat, that was saying a lot.

Thank You, God, for putting this wonderful woman in my path.

One he would never have paid attention to if she hadn't literally gotten sick at his feet. He wanted to see her. To dash out of the house and show up at her doorstep.

Now's the time to lean into the Word. The enemy likes to find little footholds in our lives and then turn them into strongholds.

Levi's words drifted into his mind, urging caution. Cameron pushed the covers away and sat up in bed, reaching for his Bible that was on the bedside table.

His relationship with Mackenzie was a delicate bloom that

needed to be protected. There were many things that could go wrong.

He could find out she was playing a role as Sylvia had been… no, he didn't believe that of Mackenzie, who hadn't been able to convincingly play the role of her twin.

No. But miscommunication and misunderstanding always lay in wait to destroy relationships.

One of them could decide they weren't right for the other. Or things petered out through no fault of their own. His relationship with Mackenzie was worth fighting for and since he didn't have the skills or the resources, he would turn it over to Someone who did.

Fortified after his morning devotion, Cameron got ready for his day. Was it too early to show up at Mackenzie's? Had she been able to get up in time for work?

Cameron groaned. He shouldn't have kept her up so late. He should have insisted she go to bed sooner. Would he never stop being an ogre who demanded people do things his way?

His phone buzzed with an incoming call. Mackenzie. A grin split his face. Maybe she was thinking of him as much as he was thinking of her.

"Hello." His pleasure at her call dropped his voice a few octaves.

Her invitation to accompany her to an auction made his smile widen until he feared his face would split.

"Let's go somewhere for dinner after." He had the perfect place in mind—one where they would have privacy and he could be himself without putting Mackenzie on edge.

They'd need to talk about that. Soon. Cameron cared about her and wanted to tell everyone. He didn't want to be Incognito Cameron anymore. He wanted to announce on the front page of every newspaper that Cameron Grant was dating Mackenzie Porter.

They agreed on a time to meet and hung up. Cameron stroked his chin. How was he supposed to dress in formal wear while concealing who he was? Worse, he had no suits in the vicinity.

Could he have Vivian send something to him? He checked the time. Nope. He had an hour before he needed to pick Mackenzie up. He'd have to solve his own problem.

* * *

Cameron let out a low whistle when Mackenzie opened the door.

"Ms. Porter, you're not playing fair. You should register that dress as a weapon." His eyes roamed over the black dress that clung to her lithe frame. She'd swept her hair into an elegant updo and slathered something glittery on her lips.

She ran her hand down her thigh and Cameron allowed himself one more second to admire her figure before he met her gaze.

"Where are your glasses?"

"Oh. I'm wearing contacts today."

"Hmm. I'll miss them." He held out a hand. "Shall we go?"

"Sure." She locked the door behind her. "Where did you get the suit?"

He smirked. "From your friends at the department store. I've proven your theory to be correct."

"Theory?" She quirked a brow.

He opened the SUV door for her, waited until she'd settled in, and put on her seatbelt.

"I may or may not have been influenced to buy a set of plaid pajamas."

Her peal of laughter followed him into the car. He was still grinning when his phone rang.

"Hello."

His mother's frosty tone curdled the smile on his face.

"Mother. To what do I owe this honor?"

Irene Grant preferred for her assistant to speak with Vivian—trusting the two women to pass her edicts on.

"If you hadn't told your assistant to stonewall me, this call wouldn't be necessary."

Cameron pinched the bridge of his nose. "What is it, Mother?"

Since his parents only called when they wanted something, it was a given. Thankfully, his mother didn't believe in subtlety or subterfuge.

"Tomorrow night is our annual Christmas party. Be here at five."

"I won't be there."

"Nonsense. The party is a Grant event. Of course, you'll be in attendance."

"Mother—" he snapped off the rest of what he was going to say. It would have been pointless as his mother had hung up. Anger and hurt warred within him. Why couldn't he have parents who loved him? Who called to check how he was doing rather than to further their own agendas?

He rested his head on the headrest, fists clenched against his thighs. And why did Mackenzie have to be here for this?

"I'm sorry." He concentrated on taking deep, calming breaths. "I'll get us there on time. Promise."

It would be a few minutes before the anger faded to a

manageable level. He wasn't about to drive in this state of agitation, not with Mackenzie in the car.

Mackenzie rested her hand on his. He flipped his hand until he was cupping hers. His anger dissipated, and he sighed.

"Want to talk about it?"

He rolled his head to study her. "My mother has ordered me to show up at the family ball tomorrow. I'd wanted to spend Christmas Eve with you."

He'd planned for an intimate evening of food and their favorite Christmas movies. An early Christmas present for him, since he'd be alone on the actual day, expecting Mackenzie to spend it with her twin.

"I've never gone to a Christmas ball."

He searched her gaze. Was she saying…? "Would you go with me?"

"Yes."

"Are you sure?" He shifted on the seat, tilting his body toward hers. "You understand I couldn't be Incognito Cameron, right?"

She nodded.

"And that there might be—will be—reporters there?"

His mother never missed a chance for what she called positive press. While his father's marriages and divorces always made headlines, Irene leaned in the other direction. She strove to get photo ops for charities and good deeds.

She cleared her throat. "I understand."

His mind raced as he pondered the implications.

She peered at him, a frown marring her features. "Don't you want me there?"

"Yes! I'd go anywhere with you." It was true. This woman was becoming his world.

"Then why are you arguing with me?"

Excellent question. While he was ready to immerse himself in her world, he wasn't sure he wanted to expose her to the toxicity of his.

"I understand how much keeping our relationship secret means to you. If you come with me to the ball, they'll link our names in the press. People will ask about you…"

He grimaced as another scenario occurred to him.

"My mother is not a nice person. Neither is my father." Accepting that had gone a long way to temper his expectations of his parents.

"Your father will be there?"

Cameron shrugged. "He might. Along with whoever he's married to or dating." The tinge of bitterness in his voice was a familiar friend. "It depends on what narrative my parents are presenting."

Cameron stayed out of their business, not wanting the taint of it to stain his own. Not that he'd wanted a life outside of his career. Until Mackenzie.

"Let me do this for you."

Her soft voice stole under his defenses.

"Why?"

"You need somebody to show up for you. No questions asked. Let me be that person for you."

Twenty-One

Chapter 21

Mackenzie waited until Cameron had parked before she spoke.

"You don't have to do this."

He turned to her. "I know, but this is my last chance to be Incognito Cameron, and I intend to make the most of it."

She raked her gaze over him. The navy blue suit made his gray eyes appear blue. "Hmm, not sure how you'll pull that off today."

He held up a finger. "First, you start with a pair of glasses." He slid on a pair of mirrored sunglasses. "Then you add a hat."

He reached into the backseat and grabbed a Fedora, plopping it onto his head. "See?"

Cameron in a Fedora did all kinds of things to her. Or maybe that was the effect of Cameron.

"Very nice." Her words came out breathy.

"You like it?"

"Oh, yes." She tilted the hat to a rakish angle. "It suits you."

"Good. I'll get your door." Cameron hurried out of the vehicle, slamming the door behind him. Mackenzie used the precious seconds to catch her breath.

Lord, I'm not sure what You meant when You asked me to be his family, but I hope You had something more permanent in mind.

Cameron helped her from the van and took her hand. Mackenzie scanned the parking lot as they approached Grady's Auction House. Not too many vehicles—that either meant the crowd hadn't come yet or most people were bidding online because of the upcoming holiday.

The two-story cream and brown building had been decorated for Christmas with red and green garlands. Tiny gold bells hung at intervals.

She stepped into the foyer and picked up a catalog. Christmas carols played through hidden speakers and the smell of cookies pervaded the air. Mackenzie grinned. She'd forgotten about this aspect of an auction at Grady's.

The auction house also boasted a bakery that sold seasonal baked goods throughout the year. The owner often joked that food and music got people in the mood to spend money.

"Come on." She tugged on Cameron's hand, pulling him deeper into the auction house. "They make the best Christmas cookies."

She made a beeline toward the concessionaire. Mackenzie skimmed the menu board, although she always got the white chocolate with macadamia nuts and cranberries.

"What do you want?"

"Is this another one of those 'I can only have what you want' moments?"

She feigned innocence. "Of course not. You can have

whatever you like. But choose wisely. This moment could make or break our relationship."

She injected levity into her tone. The corner of his mouth tilted up.

"Is that so?"

She nodded with faux solemnity as she joined the line. "Yup. A person's cookie choice has a lot to say about them."

He peered at the menu, stroking his chin. After several moments, he sighed. "This might be a death knell for us, but I'm going with the chocolate cheesecake."

She beamed up at him. How had she ever considered this man aloof?

"I take it from your response that I passed the test."

"With flying colors." She placed their order with a server wearing an elf costume. "There was no wrong answer. Unless you'd ordered one of those sweet and salty combinations." She mock-shuddered. "Who wants that level of confusion in their mouth?"

Cameron chuckled. "Do you have to stay all day?"

She flipped through the catalog. "No. The sets we want are pretty close to each other and are among the first pieces to be auctioned."

Usually, she'd stay until the end if something caught her eye. Not today. As soon as she bid on the pieces her family had earmarked, they were leaving.

"Good." He traced the curve of her ear.

"Did you have something planned?"

"I need to buy you a dress."

Mackenzie was glad when the server beckoned her. She stepped away from him and collected their cookies. Was everything about money for him? She moved at a clipped pace toward the room where her auction would be. If only her legs were longer.

"Mackenzie." Cameron caught up with her in seconds, stepping in front of her to stop her progress. He rested his hands on her shoulders. With her hands holding the bag with their cookies and two bottles of water, she couldn't push him away. But she didn't have to look at him.

"Hey," he dipped his knees to meet her gaze. "Would you look at me, please?"

She kept her chin angled away from him.

"Please." He gently turned her face toward his. She hated those mirrored glasses because he could read her expression, but they shielded his eyes from her. As if he'd read her mind, he snatched off the glasses, tucking them inside his jacket.

"Talk to me. Did I say something to offend you?"

She glared up at him. "Why does everything come down to money with you?"

His brow furrowed in confusion. "What?"

She glanced around, checking if anyone was paying attention to them.

"I don't need you to buy me things, Cameron. Believe it or not, I can dress myself. I've been doing it for over two decades."

His gaze raked her figure. "Yes, and have been doing a fantastic job."

She sighed. How was she supposed to be mad at him when he looked at her with desire and admiration?

"Then what's the problem? Why can't I wear something I already own?"

It was his turn to sigh. "Have you seen pictures of the event?"

She had. The women wore elaborate designer gowns. Some wore enough diamonds and precious gems to equip a high-end jewelry store.

"Do you have anything that wouldn't make you feel at a disadvantage among them?"

She shook her head. He cupped her face.

"I want you to be comfortable. Let me buy you an outfit. One that will make you feel and look like the princess you are."

"Laying it on kind of thick, aren't you?" She hoped her comment would distract his single-minded focus from her. The way he was staring at her made her feel…special.

"Kenzie, when will you believe I'm not trying to change you? You're perfect the way you are—whether you're the girl next door, the sexy librarian, or the polished beauty. Tomorrow, I'll present you to the world as my girlfriend. Let's make that as impactful as possible."

"Your girlfriend?" She raised stunned eyes to his. "Is that what I am to you?"

A smile played at the corners of his lips. "That's how I think of you. It's what I'd like you to be."

"Okay, Cameron." She smiled up at him. "I'll let my boyfriend buy me a dress."

Twenty-Two

Chapter 22

Cameron's fingers flew across the keypad of his phone as he arranged everything for their impromptu trip to Portsville. Doing it himself confirmed that Vivian was worth her weight in gold. This year, he would do something for her beyond the usual end-of-year bonus.

He glanced at Mackenzie. Maybe she'd help him pick out a gift for her. No. Vivian was his assistant and had been for ten years. If he paid attention to her as a person, he ought to figure out a gift that conveyed his appreciation.

Mackenzie's paddle went up, and he tuned in to the auction. "What is that?"

He'd lost track of what lot was being presented.

"It's an entryway table."

"A piece your family wants to acquire?"

"No."

"Good. It's an ugly table."

Why did people carve skulls and faces on perfectly good furniture?

Mackenzie sniffed. "It's from the Gothic era. It would be lovely in that space I cleared near the front of the store."

What Mackenzie had accomplished in a little over a week was nothing short of miraculous. She'd gotten rid of the clutter, rearranged the store, and polished the antique pieces until they glowed.

Instead of a graveyard for discarded furniture, the store had become a showcase. One that invited customers to come inside and gave them a glimpse of how the piece may look in their homes. He hoped her family appreciated it.

"In that case…" Cameron raised his paddle.

"Stop that." Mackenzie elbowed him. "You're driving up the price."

He waggled his brows. "I know."

"What are you planning to do with that ugly table?"

Her voice was huffy and Cameron bit back a grin.

"I'm not buying it." He tipped his chin toward a stern-faced woman who was glaring at him. "But she might."

The woman's paddle was up before he'd finished speaking.

"That's it. I'm out." Mackenzie dropped her paddle in her lap with a disgruntled sigh.

He grinned at her. "Then my work here is done." He lowered his paddle.

The auctioneer panned the crowd. "Does anyone want to increase the bid by one hundred?"

No one responded. The auctioneer looked at Cameron. "Sir?"

Cameron shook his head.

"Sold!" The auctioneer bellowed, "To Bidder 499."

The stern-faced woman would be happy. She'd doubtless relish having a tale about how she'd fought for the privilege of owning the Gothic entryway table.

"That should have been mine."

Mackenzie pouted. Was it wrong to be this attracted to a woman's lips? He forced himself to concentrate on the issue at hand.

"Oh, stop being a baby. There's a much better one coming up in a few lots." He flipped through the catalog and showed it to her. "It starts at a lower bid than that one and there are no creepy faces to contend with."

Her face lit. "Ooh, you're right. This is much better." She leaned over and kissed him on the cheek. "Thank you."

Cameron's heart pounded. Was it possible to fall in love with someone in a week? Because he was a goner.

* * *

Mackenzie had won the bids for two of the three pieces she'd wanted. Cameron settled her in the SUV before taking his place behind the steering wheel. It had dropped a few degrees while they'd been inside, so he turned on the engine to warm the interior.

"Let's get something to eat before we drive to Idlewood for your dress."

"I thought we'd go to Howards."

He snorted. "No."

Mackenzie worried her bottom lip. He rested a hand on hers.

"We talked about this."

"It's silly, but," Mackenzie's gaze dropped to their joint hands.

"No one except my family has ever bought me a gift."

Cameron swallowed as the implications settled in.

"I'm not sure how comfortable I am with the idea." She met his gaze, a hint of sadness in its depths. "Suppose we don't work out. What happens then?"

The idea of not being with Mackenzie twisted his gut. He wanted forever with her. He wanted to make his home with her and one day have a family. But this wasn't about him.

"I'm not the type of guy who keeps an accounting of gifts. Anything I buy for you is yours to keep. If—" he clenched his jaw, unclenched it. "If you decide this isn't what you want, then you can do whatever you want with those gifts."

He wanted to make it clear. It would *never* be his idea to break up with her, not the way he felt about her. She filled his entire world and made him see things in a new way.

He cupped her cheeks. "You're the woman I want, Mackenzie, and I'm prepared to fight for you. If you're not ready, I'll wait until you are."

Chapter 23

Mackenzie sneaked peeks at Cameron. She'd never had a guy willing to fight for her before. Or one who'd been prepared to wait. She'd had guys ask her out, but usually, when she refused, they'd backed off.

No one had ever pursued her the way Cameron had. No one had ever stuck around long enough to find out what she wanted or how they could help.

They'd stopped for Chinese and though Cameron had pretended everything was fine, a wall had gone up between them. Her fault. Why had she mentioned breaking up?

She'd only agreed to be his girlfriend moments ago. Agreed to meet his family and put their relationship into the open.

"Ugh."

Cameron glanced at her before returning his attention to the road. "Everything okay?"

"I'm an idiot."

The corner of his mouth quirked up. "Careful what you say about my girl."

Her heart thrilled at his words. "Am I still your girl?"

His gaze flickered to hers. "Of course. I meant what I said, Kenzie. You're worth fighting for."

She stared unseeing out the window. How had she gotten to this place where she was yearning for a happy ending with someone who was so far out of her league?

"We're here."

Cameron's low voice jerked her out of her thoughts. Mackenzie blinked. Cameron had parked in front of a building resembling a fairy tale cottage. The words Ella's Boutique written in an elegant script seemed to jump off the sign.

She whirled, but Cameron was already out of the vehicle. He opened the door, and she gaped at him.

"Is she the same Ella who designed the wedding dress for Princess Leilah?"

Cameron nodded, and Mackenzie suppressed a shriek. The Jazirat Aljanan princess had fallen in love with her bodyguard. Their wedding had been one of the most exciting things to happen on Saturn Island. Cameron's eyes met hers.

"Is this okay? I figured this would be better than..."

She brushed her finger over one of his eyebrows. "This is perfect."

Wait until she told Madison she had a dress designed by the famous seamstress. The door flew open at their approach. A pretty, petite woman who looked no older than a college student ran out into the parking lot at full speed.

"Cameron." She threw herself into his arms.

"Ella-Bella." Cameron caught her and swung her around. White-hot jealousy blazed through Mackenzie. She clenched her fists. Otherwise, she'd snatch the dressmaker's hands off Cameron. The two of them beamed at each other.

Mackenzie gaped at Cameron. He had never acted this way before. Did she *know* who Cameron Grant was?

Before this encounter with Ella, she'd have said yes. Now, she wasn't sure. She was about to stomp back to the truck when Ella smiled at her.

"Hello." She pulled away from Cameron with one last glance filled with fondness. "Forgive my poor manners. I'm Ella."

The pixie extended her hand. Mackenzie stared at it as if were a snake, manners and jealousy warring for dominance. Manners won. She pressed the tips of Ella's fingers.

"Hello."

Years of practice and experience dealing with clients who treated her with animosity helped her keep her smile on her face. Barely.

Ella scanned her from head to toe. "You're right, Cameron, she's gorgeous. I have the perfect dress for her. I designed it for someone with a similar figure."

Being called gorgeous by this beautiful woman did nothing to calm Mackenzie's raging blood. Nor did the prospect of owning an Ella original.

"How do you two know each other?"

The normalcy of her voice surprised her. Cameron and Ella beamed at each other. Mackenzie gritted her teeth. Hadn't he claimed *she* was his girl? If so, how did he explain Ella?

"Uh." Cameron massaged the back of his neck. "Ella is my..." He looked at the younger woman.

"Cameron and I are...hmm." Ella pursed her lips. "We've never had to define our relationship before."

Relationship? The two of them had a relationship?

Mackenzie's tenuous grasp on her patience—and her temper— snapped.

"If you're telling me she's your ex, just say it!"

The abject horror on both of their faces cued her in that something was off. Ella was the first to recover.

"Eww." She mock-shuddered. "Cameron and I have never dated, and never will. It would be like dating my brother."

Was she telling the truth? Mackenzie studied their faces. Cameron's mouth curved down.

"I would never take you to meet an ex-girlfriend without warning you." He hurried to clasp her elbows, peering down into her eyes.

Ella giggled. "Not that you have many."

"Shut up, squirt." Cameron threw an affectionate glower over his shoulder. Mackenzie figured it out then and her cheeks warmed.

"Are you two related?"

"Uhm," Cameron hedged. "Not exactly."

Ella smacked him on the arm with such force that Mackenzie felt the vibration.

"Our parents were married for a second." Ella scrunched up her nose. "Cam was twelve, and I was—"

"A pain in my neck. She followed me everywhere."

Ella threw up her hands. "I was bored, and you were at least somewhat interesting."

Cameron picked up the story. "We kept in touch after the divorce and now I can't get rid of her."

The affection in his voice was evident. Mackenzie's cheeks warmed. Would she forever embarrass herself in front of this man?

She'd accused him of bringing her to meet his ex-girlfriend.

She'd been standoffish and rude to her dream designer when the woman was Cameron's honorary sister. Mackenzie flicked a glance to Ella. The woman smirked. She would never live this down.

"Ella, can you give us a minute?"

"Sure." Amusement colored Ella's voice. "I'll be around the back when you're ready."

The second Ella was out of earshot, Mackenzie began apologizing. "I'm sorry. I don't—"

"Shh." A light brush of his lips against her forehead cut off the flow of words. "You have nothing to be sorry for. I should have handled that better."

He pulled back, lips pressed into a wry smile. "I wanted to impress you by showing off my impressive connections. Remind me never to do that again."

He was trying to impress her?

"Why?"

At his confused frown, she tried again. "Why would you need to impress me?"

He gaped at her. "Are you kidding me? Do you know how hard I've been trying to keep your attention? Usually, I'd go all out when I'm dating someone, but you won't let me buy you a cup of soup." He made a face. "It's humbling and a little scary."

Did he not recognize how much he had to offer? He was more than his assets in the bank. Though he hid it well, his heart was pure. She cupped his face, drawing his attention back to her.

"I see you, Cameron Grant," she placed a hand over his heart, "and I'm impressed."

Twenty-Four

Chapter 24

"Ready?"

Cameron tried to read Mackenzie's expression, but she'd followed his instructions a little too well. Her navy pantsuit and smooth bun reminded him of the woman who'd kept him at arm's length. Shades hid her eyes, and she was once again in professional hostess mode.

She'd hooked her dress bag over her rolling suitcase to prevent damage to the fabric. Admiration for her beat back the fear that came from thrusting an innocent into his world. Almost.

Had he done the right thing by inviting her here? Maybe he should have ignored his mother's summons and remained in Cinnamon Hill. Or maybe he should have come on his own. He'd have been back with Mackenzie early on Christmas morning.

A cool hand brushed his. "It will be okay. I'm not as fragile as I appear."

"Is it bad that I want to protect you from everything, including my mother?"

Her lips curved. "Unless she has a poisoned apple or a magic spindle, I'll be fine."

"She might."

Her peal of laughter made him regret they were in an airport terminal. He wanted to capture her lips with his, but he resisted the urge. The airport wasn't as crowded as it would be later that day, but all it took was one overeager person with a cell phone. Then, the news that he was traveling with a guest would get to Irene Grant before he could tell her.

She hadn't been the best mother in the world, but she deserved a personal introduction to the woman he was hoping to marry. If he could convince Mackenzie to stick around long enough.

"Our ride's here." He tipped his chin toward a young man in a black suit holding a sign with his surname.

Cameron settled beside Mackenzie in the back of the Mercedes while the driver took care of the bags. Once on the road, the driver kept his gaze fixed on the road. For once, Cameron was glad to give up the control. He was free to concentrate on Mackenzie while someone else battled the holiday traffic.

"Where are we going?"

He took one of her hands in his. "To my mother's house, where I'll introduce you to her. After that, I'd like to have lunch with you."

They'd opted to fly in early to beat the crowds and the worst of the traffic. But there was no way he wanted to spend any more time with his mother than necessary.

The vehicle drove up the cobblestone driveway and parked

in front of the house.

Mackenzie gaped. "You grew up here?"

"Yes." Cameron kept his gaze on her. Was this where he lost her? Because this house would seem excessive to Mackenzie. A hotel-sized residence for a family of three—two after his father had left.

"Did you need a map?" She smirked at him. "Because I'll need one. And a compass. Maybe a GPS system?"

Her teasing tone lightened his apprehension. He leaned over and kissed her on the cheek. "I don't deserve you, Mackenzie, but I'm glad you're here."

This might be the first Christmas party he enjoyed in years.

* * *

"Ena, this is Mackenzie," he grinned down at her. "My girlfriend."

He looked back at the housekeeper and caught the widening of her eyes.

"Your mother won't be happy."

Irene Grant rarely was. The plump woman who'd been with his family since he'd been a boy leaned closer, her voice dropping to a whisper. "She had plans for you." She fluttered her hands. "Girls coming from all over the place—as if this was a game show."

His jaw clenched. Was that why Irene had insisted he come to the party this year? Because there was a woman she wanted to foist on him? Who would it be this time? The daughter of some politician she wanted to align herself with? Or some debutante whose family lived up to Irene's standards?

Mackenzie's hand brushed against his, and he clung to it like a lifeline.

"Is she here?" He held on to his temper because of long years of practice.

Ena's eyes widened. "No, sir. She and the girls went out a few hours ago. They're having a spa day."

The housekeeper's words registered.

"You said 'girls'. Who did my mother invite?"

"Rachel Andrews, Angela Smith, and Suzanne Scott."

His eyes widened at the names—each woman was the daughter of a man her mother sought alliances with. Though she no longer ran the company, as a major shareholder, she was always trying to have things done her way. Maybe it was time to part ways with the family business.

Mackenzie's fingers tightened on his. "Everything okay?"

"No." He nodded to Ena. "Change of plans. Please don't tell Mother I was here."

"Where are you going?" Ena's voice pitched upward.

"I'll be back this evening."

He pivoted on his heel, tugging Mackenzie along with him, glad he'd asked the driver to wait. He handed Mackenzie into the vehicle before stashing their bags in the trunk. Cameron gave the driver an address and settled beside Mackenzie, resting his head against the back of the seat.

"What just happened?" Mackenzie tipped her head toward the house. "Who were those women? Wasn't the plan for me to stay at the house?"

Her questions came faster the longer he remained silent. He took her hand, interlocking his fingers with hers.

"If this was fifty years earlier, my mother would have married me to one of those women. To her, it's all about increasing wealth. It has nothing to do with the people involved."

That had been his father's terrible sin. Not the cheating or multiple partners, but that he'd dared to divorce her, resulting in a division of assets and a recalculation of their wealth.

"I didn't want to leave you at the house with those women."

Mackenzie smiled. "I can hold my own against mean girls."

He brushed a finger over her ear, needing the contact. "I don't doubt it. But the last time my mother did something similar, only one woman showed up for dinner. One dress somehow ended up in the pool and the others in little shreds."

Mackenzie blinked. "These are the women your mother has determined would be suitable matches for you?" Her smile was sympathetic. "She doesn't know you well, does she?"

"No."

Yet the woman beside him had uncovered many of his secrets in a short time. Maybe it was because, with her, he could be himself without all the layers he relied on for protection. With Mackenzie, he wanted to lay himself bare because he trusted her to keep his heart safe.

Chapter 25

⸎

Was this what life was like for Cameron? A constant reminder that everyone wanted something from him? Even his mother considered him a pawn—something to be used to further her own interests.

This was why God had asked her to show him what it meant to have a family. Because though her father didn't understand her vision for the antique shop, she had always known her parents loved her.

Lord, please show Cameron how valuable he is to You. Show him how much You love and care for him.

She regarded him out of the corner of her eye, pretending to be engrossed in the scenery. His earlier despondence simmered under the surface as his fingers flew over the keypad of his phone. How could she draw him out of his current mood?

She tapped her chin as an idea occurred to her. She sighed

melodramatically. As she'd hoped, his head snapped up.

"Are you okay?"

"I had a glimpse into my future."

"Oh?" He raised an eyebrow. "That bad?"

"Yes. I foresaw many trips similar to this one. I sat beside my husband, craving his attention while he was busy with his phone."

Cameron pocketed the phone. "This husband of yours is a fool." He stretched his arm against the back of the seat and turned the full force of his gray gaze on her. "Tell me who this fool is. I want to teach him a lesson."

Oh. Why had she started this line of conversation? Her eyes flitted to his lips and back. Was he closer than before?

"Uhm. It was hard to see his face." Not a lie, but she wanted it to be him.

"That's good. Then I can put in my application."

Her breath caught. "Application?"

What on earth were they talking about?

"For the position of your husband."

He *had* been moving closer. He was close enough for her to smell the mint on his breath. For her to count the lines around his irises.

The vehicle pulled to a stop.

"We're here."

The driver's voice was unassuming, but Mackenzie's cheeks burned. She'd been so caught up in Cameron she'd forgotten about him.

Cameron leaned in. "To be continued."

His warm breath caused a shiver of delicious anticipation to run down her spine. She hoped next time she'd get to taste his lips. To find out if what had happened the first time had been a fluke. Or if kissing Cameron generated enough heat to keep her warm for several winters.

Mackenzie frowned when she spotted the sign of the exclusive hotel. Her head whipped around to Cameron.

"Why are we here?"

Tension radiated off him. "I got you a room. Since staying at the house is no longer an option, you need a place to stash your luggage and get ready for this evening."

"Where are you staying?"

He shrugged. "I have an apartment in town. I'll get ready there."

She arched a brow.

"No. Staying with me is out of the question. It would have been okay at the house because my mother and half a dozen other people would have been there."

He had a point, but she disliked having him spend money on her. She hated that a part of her brain was calculating the cost and figuring out how long she'd have to work to pay for a single night.

"Mackenzie." He ran a finger down her cheek and she hissed out a breath as electricity followed its path. "Please let me do this for you. While we're in Portsville, let me spoil you a little. I promise to go back to being Incognito Cameron the second we're back in Cinnamon Hill."

He was coming back with her? A smile stole over her face. A man willing to embrace a simpler lifestyle for her deserved a chance to spoil her.

"Just a little." She held her thumb and pointer fingers an inch apart.

"Thank you." He rested his forehead against hers for a second before pulling back. "The reservation is under your name.

Collect the key at the front desk."

"You're not coming in with me?"

He shook his head. "Not after I've gone to so much trouble to secure your reputation. In this town, something doesn't need to have an inkling of truth for it to be believed by the masses."

He brushed a thumb over her cheek. "I'll wait for you in the lobby. Then we'll go out for lunch."

* * *

Sheer willpower kept her from gawking as she walked through the polished hotel into the elevator. The gold elevator had a seat—a comfy sofa that belonged in someone's living room.

The liveried bellhop smiled at her. "Room number?"

She glanced at the key fob and reeled off the number.

"Ah, the penthouse. I believe you will be happy with the accommodations."

The penthouse? When she'd agreed Cameron could foot the bill for the hotel, she'd expected a regular room, but the penthouse? It was too much.

The elevator doors slid open, and she stepped into the tiled walkway, following the bellhop to the suite. Everything gleamed.

She turned in a complete circle, eyes darting over the features. Waterfall chandelier. Cream and black were the dominant colors, with gold accents. The result was an elegant, if somewhat masculine, space.

The young man refused her attempts to tip him and left Mackenzie to ogle the room. If she'd considered Cameron's plane luxurious, she was mistaken. Every piece of furniture invited her to stay awhile and let them pamper her.

Her house, her parents' house, and the antique shop could fit into the suite with room left over. What was she supposed to do with all this space?

She wandered to the glass walls and peered out. This high up, everything appeared smaller and cleaner somehow. As if the elevation had cut away the problems and stress of the world.

She shook her head to dispel the notion. This wasn't her life—this illusion of ease and safety.

Do you want it to be?

She ignored the tiny voice.

Cameron was waiting. She moved her luggage to a corner of the living room, trailing her finger over the handle. She and Cameron had a lot to talk about.

Chapter 26

What would he do about his mother? Cameron drummed his fingers against the arm of the comfortable couch as he waited for Mackenzie's return.

Irene Grant's desire to marry him off to a woman of her choosing had never been a secret. But for her to invite, not one, but three women to the annual ball—a ball she'd insisted he attend—hinted at something deeper.

She couldn't force him to marry, and for that, he was thankful. Still, it would be in his best interest—and Mackenzie's—to figure out what her goal was.

He took out his phone to make a quick call to his mother, though she hated being disturbed on her spa days. He paused when he spotted Mackenzie coming toward him. The storm in her eyes told him he had more immediate troubles to handle.

He stood. Better to meet this tempest head-on. She jerked

to a stop in front of him, plopping her hands on her hips.

"The penthouse suite is not a little spoiling."

He bit back a grin. What would she say if she suspected how much he held back from showering her with gifts?

"It was all they had."

She opened her mouth, then snapped it shut, eyes darting back and forth between his. He tugged her hands off her hips, clasping them in his.

"Truly. It's Christmas Eve." He gestured to the lobby that was decked in Christmas colors for the holiday. The huge artificial tree spiraled toward the ceiling, lights twinkling in muted splendor.

"Plus, my mother's guests have taken a lot of the rooms in the local hotels. Her annual Christmas party is quite the thing around here."

She was quick to mask her anxiety, but he caught it in the tightening of her lips—in the way her eyes refused to meet his. Probably because her face was becoming as familiar to him as his own.

"Say the word, and we'll make a flight plan to return to Cinnamon Hill today."

She sagged against him, resting her head against his chest. He cradled her against him, careful not to crush her. Why did this woman cause such a myriad of emotions to wash over him?

"I'm afraid I'll mess things up. That you'll assume I'm some kind of gold digger who's after your money."

Her voice was muffled, but he heard every word. He felt them as though someone had carved them into his flesh. He pressed her away from him, dipping his knees until he was staring into her eyes.

"Never." He cupped her face in his hands. "Mackenzie, I would never believe that of you. I meant what I said earlier. Let me treat you while we're here. Tomorrow we can go back to being us."

"Promise?"

Her voice was husky with emotion. The moment was heavy with meaning. An image flashed into his mind. He and Mackenzie sat on an old couch in his uncle's house, cuddling. He had a sense of warmth and love. The image was gone in a second, replaced with him standing alone in the apartment he kept in town. A sense of loneliness and despair flooded through him.

The stark difference between the two images said more than if someone had tried to express the same sentiments in a thousand words. He'd trade every cent of his wealth if he got to spend the rest of his life with Mackenzie.

"Promise."

Why were they having this conversation in public? He wanted to seal his promise with a kiss. To use his lips to impress upon her the depth of his sincerity. Instead, mindful of their audience, he pressed a chaste kiss to her forehead. It would have to do.

* * *

Cameron studied Mackenzie as they turned off the main road onto the airstrip. She'd been subdued. Maybe she was suppressing her independent streak at least a little, so he could spoil her today.

"Where are we?" She glanced at the single helicopter that waited on the tarmac, then back at him. "Why are we here?"

"Do you trust me?" He held out his hand.

Please let her say yes.

Her eyes met his. "Of course."

She slipped her hand into his and Cameron's breath whooshed out. He assisted her out of the car, hustling toward the helicopter, ducking his head as he assisted her in. He motioned to the headset. What was she thinking? Did she like it? Was this too extravagant?

"Are you alright?"

She nodded, eyes fixed on the view outside. Within minutes, they were airborne, whisking through the air. It wouldn't take long to get to their destination, but Cameron took the time to pray.

Please, God, let everything turn out how I envisioned it. Don't let me lose her with this display of wealth.

Why was she opposed to money? Or was it *his* money she had a problem with?

He'd been born into a wealthy family. He'd never lacked physical things. Could he be with someone who couldn't accept every aspect of who he was?

"Is that where we're going?" Mackenzie pointed through the window to a large white boat that sat in the middle of the sea.

He leaned closer to her, though he saw what she was pointing at.

"Yes." He inhaled, filling his lungs with her sweet citrus scent.

She twisted her head in his direction, and for a second, her lips distracted him. They were so close to his.

"You own a boat?"

He searched her eyes. "Would you like me to?"

Her eyes revealed nothing. Cameron sighed.

"No. It's a floating restaurant. I thought you'd enjoy the

experience." And the privacy since he'd rented the boat for a few hours.

"I've never been on a boat before." A tiny smile played around the corner of her mouth. Cameron sighed in relief. It would be okay.

An hour later, Cameron sat across from Mackenzie, empty dishes splayed between them. She'd chosen a table beside a window overlooking the ocean. The blue of the water as it met the bright blue of the sky gave the impression they were in a bubble. Soft Christmas music played in the background.

"Did you enjoy your meal?"

"Hmm." She used a warm, damp towel to wipe her hands and mouth. "Best jerk chicken I've had in a while." Mischief crept over her face. "But not as good as the one in Orange Valley."

He burst out laughing. "You would say that."

"I don't understand something." She scrunched up her nose.

"What's that?"

"Why is this restaurant empty on Christmas Eve?"

"Uhm." Every thought fled from his mind. What was he supposed to say? He didn't want to lie to her, but what could he say that wouldn't put her back on the defensive?

She patted his hand. "How hard has it been to resist spending a lot of money in the last couple of days?"

His breath whooshed out. She wasn't mad. "It's the most difficult thing I've ever had to do."

"Thank you."

Was she thanking him for spending money or for not spending it?

"Why does my taking care of you bother you?"

She dropped her eyes to the table, playing with the edge of her napkin. "I don't have a problem with your money,

Cameron. Not exactly. But people with money sometimes behave as if it gives them permission to erode the rights of others. I don't want that for myself."

"And you believe I would do that?"

"No." Her fingers tightened around his. "I get that your wealth is part of the package, Cameron. Be patient with me as I work on being okay with it."

He didn't receive the heartfelt acceptance he wanted, but it was enough. For now. She was making room for all parts of him in her life. God had heard his prayer and was working on softening her heart.

Thank You, Lord. Please don't let me mess up.

Twenty-Seven

Chapter 27

Mackenzie met the gaze of the middle-aged woman in the mirror. Within an hour after she'd returned to the hotel, Brandy had shown up with her daughter, Fiona. They had worked a miracle on her hair and makeup.

At first, she'd been uncomfortable sitting before the two women wearing the plush robe from the bathroom. The genuine niceness of the women soon overcame her reservations.

"Okay, love," Brandy's voice had a rhythmic cadence, a testament that she'd lived at least part of her life on one of the islands surrounding Saturn Island. "Now all you gotta do is put on your dress. Do you need help?"

Did she? Ella had helped her with the dress the first time and then had flitted around as if she was a mother hen. Mackenzie bit the corner of her lip.

"Hey," Fiona yelled. "Don't you dare mess up my handiwork."

"Sorry." Mackenzie apologized, though she doubted the deepest kiss would smudge the tint on her lips. Her cheeks warmed. Why was she thinking about kissing? "Do you mind?"

"Of course not, sweetie." Brandy waved a hand. "You get your dress and we'll help you get ready for your date."

She hurried to the closet and, with shaking hands, unzipped the garment bag. With the women's help, she stepped into the dress. The deep fuchsia was not a color she normally wore, but the shade complemented her complexion, making it appear as if she had an inner glow. She liked it.

"Girl, you're killing it." Brandy wolf-whistled.

"Yeah, Momma. Her guy's going to swallow his tongue when he sees her."

Mackenzie's lips quirked as she studied her reflection. He might. This dress made her feel like Cinderella on her way to the ball. Let's hope she didn't turn into a pumpkin at midnight.

* * *

When the elevator door opened, she was the one who almost swallowed her tongue. Had she considered Cameron handsome in a suit? He was devastating in a tux with his fresh haircut and smooth-shaven face.

His eyes widened at her approach, lips curving in appreciation. She became shy in his presence. Somehow, tonight he wasn't her Incognito Cameron—the man she'd gotten to know as they worked together. He was Cameron Grant. Real estate dynamo. Billionaire.

"Hi."

"Hi." He mimicked her greeting. "Every time I believe you can't get any more beautiful, you do." His eyes darted to her lips before flitting back to hers. Her chest tightened at the passion that burned there.

"There'd better be lots of mistletoe tonight because I intend to steal at least one kiss."

She laughed and batted her eyes at him. "Please do. I've been dying to find out if the last kiss was a fluke."

His eyes darkened. "You are dangerous to my peace of mind, Ms. Porter."

He offered his arm, and she slipped her arm in his. And he was dangerous to her heart.

After her first ride in a limousine, Mackenzie stepped out into a whole new world. The entire building was lit up, frost lights outlining the exterior. Even the grounds were bright, the lights giving the impression it was still daylight.

She took a deep breath. Alright, Mackenzie, this is it.

Cameron turned to her, his broad shoulders shielding her from view. "You don't have to do this. Say the word and I'll whisk you away from here. We'll leave and have our own private Christmas Eve party."

His low voice thrummed with sincerity and she felt a warmth that started from within. He meant it. Cameron would walk away from the biggest event of the year and away from his mother and whoever waited for him inside. He would walk away—for her.

She rested a palm against his cheek. Cameron hissed out a breath. "Cold hands?"

"Maybe." Cameron pressed a kiss to her palm and Mackenzie forgot her next thought. "It's more of a reaction to your touch." His eyes darkened. "You've never touched me like this."

The protest bubbled up before she could temper it. "I touch you all the time."

"Hmm." He agreed. "Not like this."

He reached toward her as if to cradle her face, then chose instead to brush the lobe of her ear. Why had she agreed to wear makeup? If she hadn't, Cameron would be cupping her face, making her feel as if she was the most precious person in his world.

A flash went off and Mackenzie blinked and made to turn in the direction.

"Ignore them. Makes it easier to deal with them." A muscle ticked in his jaw.

"Hey," she drew his attention back to her. "Don't be mad." She gave him a teasing grin. "If Vivian and Edward can get through this, we can too."

"What?" His brow marred in confusion. "Vivian's in love?"

She feigned innocence. "You've never watched Pretty Woman?"

"Oh. You're talking about a movie." His brow smoothed. "For a second, I thought you were talking about my assistant."

How could she have forgotten the name of the woman who sometimes flew with Cameron?

"Not tonight." She jostled his arm to reset the mood. "Tonight it's all about Pretty Woman. It couldn't have been easy for Vivian to fit into Edward's world after they fell in love."

Cameron threw back his head and laughed. "What am I going to do with you?"

She swallowed back her first response. Love me. Spend the rest of your life making me feel like your princess.

She shrugged. "No clue."

He tucked her arms in his. "Why don't I take you to a ball?"

She nodded. It would have to be enough. No one would

believe she'd fallen in love or that she was ready to change her life to fit into his world. For him.

Those things only happen in fairy tales. She took a bracing breath, and usually, the princess had to face an ogre or a witch before she got her happy ending.

She shrugged off the whiff of forewarning. This was her first ball, and she intended to enjoy every second.

Twenty-Eight

Chapter 28

The Grants had been hosting an annual Christmas Eve ball at their country club for as long as he could remember. As a child, he'd been eager for the day when he'd be old enough to attend.

By his eighteenth birthday, he'd become jaded after realizing there was nothing Christmassy about the event. The same petty jealousies that ruled the other days of the year reigned on this day as well.

A slight tug on his arm jolted him back to the present.

"Is that Alexander Montgomery?" Mackenzie inclined her chin while keeping a serene expression. Who was this woman? He glanced in the direction she'd indicated.

"Yes."

"Are you two friends?"

"No."

"Why not?" Her curiosity drew him. "You're almost the same

age. Both of you are billionaires and he's here at your mother's party, so you have friends in common."

"Associates." He corrected her assumption automatically. There was no one in this room he considered a friend, except her. These people were business partners, associates, and sometimes enemies, but never friends.

"How sad."

She saw too much, this woman with her kind eyes and tender heart. How would she survive in this barren environment? Why should she need to?

He'd put up with it because he'd grown up among these people. But why should he subject himself to a toxic environment because it was the norm in his family?

"Let's go." He took her hand and pivoted toward the door.

"You're late." His mother blocked his exit with an icy expression. "I remember telling you I expected you at five."

He'd ignored her missive on purpose, not wanting to be seated around the dinner table while people pushed food around on their plates, pretending to eat.

"Hello, Mother." He leaned down for the obligatory air kiss.

"Who is this?" Her eyes cut to Mackenzie with curiosity and a hint of some other emotion that was too fleeting to be identified.

"This is Mackenzie." He smiled down at her, placing a hand over the one that had gone tense on his arm. "My girlfriend."

"Girlfriend?" His mother's voice was loud enough to catch the attention of the people closest to them. Shock and interest registered on most faces.

"You're overwrought. Let's talk about this someplace else." His mother made a beeline across the room, expecting him to follow.

"You should go with your mother." Mackenzie's lips curved, but the smile didn't reach her eyes.

He checked the faces closest to them. "I'm not leaving you out here alone."

He linked his fingers with hers. Cameron knew where his mother would go. She always rented this ballroom because it had a small sitting room. When they entered, Irene sat on one of the low couches, a queen granting an audience.

"What is the meaning of this?"

Cameron lifted a brow. "Isn't this what you've wanted for several months?" Years. "You've been after me to get married. Mackenzie and I are dating."

He smiled down at Mackenzie, loving the way her eyes softened when she looked at him. "Hopefully, it will lead to step thirteen." He flicked a glance at his mother. "Marriage."

Irene gave him a frosty glare, but having never received kindness from her, it had long lost its power. She turned the force of her glare on Mackenzie.

"Who are your parents?"

"Robert and Margaret Porter." Mackenzie's voice was a little strained, but it didn't break.

"What do they do?"

Her tongue darted out to wet her lips. "My family owns an antique store in Cinnamon Hill."

Irene scanned Mackenzie from head to toe. "I suppose you expect you've found a cash cow—someone you can fleece until you've stolen all his wealth?"

What? His mother had never spoken in such an abrupt manner to anyone.

"Mother—"

"No, ma'am." Mackenzie cut him off. "I don't want

Cameron's money. I can make my own."

"Oh?" Irene's gaze was cutting. "What do you do? I suppose you work in your parents' shop." Her hands flittered in dismissal.

"No, ma'am." Mackenzie tilted her chin. "I'm an air hostess."

Irene scoffed. "Really, Cameron, surely you can do better than this?" She waved a hand to encompass Mackenzie. "She's a glorified waitress."

"One who has a degree in communications and business management. I'm also a certified CPR and First Aid Trainer and am fluent in three languages. I don't need your son's money, Mrs. Grant. I can earn my own.

"Not only that," she gave him a soft smile before whipping her head back toward his mother, eyes narrowed. "I see him. Much better than you or anyone in this building."

She rested a palm on his chest. "You were right, CJ. We shouldn't be here." She stalked toward the door, head held high. Now there was a woman capable of being a queen. Was it a surprise that he loved her? He loved her.

The realization settled in his heart along with the truth that he couldn't allow his mother to ruin the first genuine relationship he'd had with a woman.

He turned to Irene. She was still gaping at the door Mackenzie had disappeared through.

"Mother." At his voice, she snapped her mouth shut.

"Are you going to let her talk to me that way?"

"You deserved it." And much worse. Her beloved Suzanne would have been cruel. Mackenzie had put his mother in her place without being rude.

"Mackenzie and I are leaving. I won't come anywhere near you if you insist on trying to run my life. I'm not a pawn in your game, Mother. I'm a grown man capable of making my own choices, including who I want to date."

"You're too young to know what you want."

He arched a brow. "May I remind you that you turned over the company to me when I was eighteen years old? That was ten years ago. "

She waved off his words. To Irene, they were inconsequential.

"I'm your mother. I know what's best for you."

He snorted. "Bringing a child into the world does not make you a mother."

His heart ached as he walked away from her, but he needed to cut ties. His desire for a healthy relationship far outweighed his need for his mother's love or her approval. He'd tried and failed to attain those things for many years. No more. This year, he was drawing a line in the sand and stepping over it.

God had been trying to show Cameron that family had nothing to do with blood and everything to do with the heart.

God wants me to show you what family is.

Thank You for opening my eyes to the treasure in front of me.

Cameron slipped his arms around Mackenzie's rigid frame, sighing when she settled into him. "It's okay, Princess. We'll be okay."

Twenty-Nine

Chapter 29

The thrill of being called Cameron's girlfriend swept over her. Until Irene Grant's dismissive response. The woman made it clear Mackenzie was not an appropriate match for Cameron.

All her insecurities came flooding back. Would the people in Cameron's world always consider her an interloper? It would be so easy to slip out the door and return to the hotel room.

Mackenzie faked a smile for Cameron so he wouldn't know how much his mother's words had hurt her.

"You should go with your mother."

Cameron glanced at the faces closest to them—people who watched with curiosity and something she couldn't name in their eyes. What were they expecting to happen?

"I'm not leaving you out here alone."

He linked his fingers with hers, and her shoulders relaxed. He still chose her. She drew strength from that as she followed

Cameron through the sea of people. Mackenzie held her head high, ignoring the curious, sometimes hostile stares.

Was this a taste of what it was like to be wealthy? The images in the newspapers or magazines conveyed glamour and exclusivity. She realized then that the photos were selected to cultivate envy.

They did not depict the loneliness and isolation that permeated the air. Did everyone in this room attend this ball out of obligation? Where were the friendships? The laughter?

Because if this had been her family's ball, laughter would have echoed through the hall. Not this jaded politeness and the sense that everyone was biding their time, staying only as long as necessary, but no one was having fun.

After standing up to his mother, it had taken all her willpower to walk out of the room with her spine straight. She waited outside the door, praying Cameron would be out before anyone approached her.

A few of the women smirked at her as if they'd been privy to the conversation. How many of them had Mrs. Grant's sharp tongue flayed?

Lord, please don't let me cower in front of these people.

She angled her chin, meeting the gazes of those sneering at her until they turned away.

Cameron slipped his arms around her. She sighed, relaxing into him. Being with him felt right. She'd face down Irene Grant a thousand times for the privilege to be in his arms like this.

"It's okay, Princess," he murmured the words close to her ear. "We'll be okay."

"I can't believe I got dressed up for this." She pulled back to meet his eyes. "Look at me. I'm on fire."

"Are you sure that's you?" Appreciation burned in his gaze until an answering warmth ignited inside her. "There's somewhere we can go."

"Yes?" She faked a bright smile. As much as what Irene had said had stung, the woman wasn't *her* mother. Cameron had lived with her. No doubt what had happened tonight had hurt him more than it had her.

"It will require an open mind."

She leaned closer. "Are we crashing a party?"

"Maybe." His eyes twinkled with mischief. He cast a glance over his shoulder. "Let's get out of here."

* * *

Mackenzie approached another luminous building on Cameron's arm. Did these people not pay for electricity?

"What is this place?"

She gawked at the Christmas tree that towered over them, laden with silver ornaments and tinsel.

"This is my country club."

"You belong to two clubs?"

"Yes. No." He pressed his lips together. "The one we're coming from is the one my parents belong to. I visit as my mother's guest. This is where my membership is."

She got it. He needed an identity away from his parents. Something that was all his.

"So we're not crashing a party, then?" She allowed a bit of disappointment to seep into her voice.

"No." He pulled her into a lobby decorated by someone who had excellent taste and enthusiasm for Christmas.

Whereas Mrs. Grant's party had been all icy colors in shades of silver and white—this ball used the more traditional colors of Christmas. Pops of green and red reminded her of home. Christmas carols played from hidden speakers.

Though the room was also large, this club was more intimate. Friendly.

"I never get to attend this Christmas ball because I'm expected to be at my mother's."

A masked employee walked up to them, carrying a basket. "A mask for you, sir?" He handed Cameron a black mask decorated with silver. "And for the lady?"

He angled the basket toward them. Cameron withdrew a turquoise and gold mask with long pink feathers the same shade as her dress.

"This one."

"Excellent choice, sir." The server nodded his assent. "This year we have a special ball for couples. If you'll follow me."

They followed him into a large ballroom—her second one for the night. Unlike the last one, there wasn't a single piece of furniture. The hardwood floor gleamed. Masked couples stood at the edges of the room.

Her eyebrows winged up. "What's going on?"

The club staff member smiled at them. "Ballroom dancing."

He made a slight bow and disappeared. She whipped her head to frown at Cameron.

"Do you dance? I don't." She'd always envied people who moved their bodies effortlessly in complex dance moves. "I have two left feet."

Cameron's eyes blazed at her. "I doubt that." Was it the mask that made the gray appear deeper? Or something else? "I've seen you move. You're as graceful as a swan."

She snorted. "Have you been watching swans, CJ?"

The nickname rolled off her tongue.

He smirked. "No, but I've been watching you. Besides," he rested his hands on her shoulders and turned her to face the dance floor. "We'll have help."

The couple in the center of the ballroom had the perfect postures of professional dancers.

Excitement frittered down her spine. She'd always wanted to learn how to dance. She tugged Cameron closer to the couple, not wanting to miss a step.

After demonstrating the waltz, the woman clapped her hands. "Now you."

Cameron pulled her into his arms, mimicking the posture and arm positions of the couple. "This couldn't be more perfect if I'd planned it."

His soft words made her lose count.

"I'm sorry?" Her breath caught as their eyes met. She stepped on his shoe. "Sorry." She winced. "I told you I wasn't good at this."

"Focus on me and follow my lead."

She locked eyes on him and allowed him to lead. She'd always considered dancing complicated, but in Cameron's arms, she floated. The background melted away until they were the only two people in the room.

Thirty

Chapter 30

Having Mackenzie in his arms was a delight. And the way she looked at him? He felt at least ten feet tall, as if he were a man worthy of her affections. He felt like someone who could shake off his past and walk into a brighter future.

Could she love him? Could she spend the rest of her life with him? Because he pictured himself with her. He imagined them making a family where the love of God and each other triumphed over the love of money and stuff. A home where people cared enough to put the other person's needs above their own.

A soft smile danced around her lips. "Those must be some deep thoughts."

Ones that would scare her away.

"Care to share?"

"Aren't you supposed to offer something for my thoughts?

Like a penny?"

She threw her head back and laughed, the sound curling around his heart.

"Why would I offer you money?"

"These are important thoughts. The least you can do is barter for them."

"What can I offer you?"

He reveled in the breathlessness of her voice, his eyes dropping to her lips.

"The best reward of all." He put his mouth near her ear, needing to be closer. "A kiss."

The music trailed off. He groaned. Mackenzie chuckled and patted his cheek.

"We'll talk about your deep thoughts later."

Another club staff member was in the center of the room, wearing green and red in honor of the season.

"Most of you were enjoying yourselves and probably wanted to continue practicing your new dance moves. You'll get plenty of time to do that later." The woman grinned. "If you choose. But it's time for us to move on to the next segment of the program."

Cameron glanced around the room. Several couples pursed their lips in displeasure. One couple kept dancing, though the music had stopped. He wasn't the only one who hadn't wanted the dance to end.

"There are Christmas elves among you." She gestured to the men and women who were drifting towards the couples, tablets, and styluses in hand. "We have assigned each couple a number. Collect your number and place your dinner orders."

Mackenzie tugged on his sleeve. "What are they talking about?"

He lifted a shoulder. "No clue." A thrill of excitement ran down his spine. "Sounds like an adventure. Are you up for it?"

"With you?" Her lips curved. "Anytime."

They collected their numbers and accepted the key to a golf cart. His eyebrow winged up. His suit wasn't appropriate attire for a game, nor was he in the mood to play golf if it had been.

"Follow the arrows." The staff member winked at them, his lopsided Santa hat giving him a mischievous air.

Mackenzie slipped her hand into his. "This is more fun than what happened at your mother's party."

As he stared at her upturned face, he had to agree, her excitement triggering his own.

There was a line of golf carts in the driveway. A lone employee stood beside them.

"Check for your number on the golf course."

This was getting weirder by the second. Should he proceed? He arched a brow at Mackenzie. She nodded, eyes bright with joy. He handed her into the cart, taking care to tuck her dress around her calves. Her strong, shapely calves…Hmm, maybe this wasn't so bad after all.

Nope, it was perfect. The tiny golf cart meant she had to press close to him on the seat, one arm around his waist as an anchor. He wanted to drive for a long, long time. Would she notice if he kept driving and never stopped?

He glanced down at Mackenzie. Excitement radiated off her as her head swiveled to take in everything. Cameron made a mental note to bring her for lunch one day so she could have the full experience.

"There are tents on the golf course." Mackenzie's voice was awed, and a little amused.

"Hmm."

Cameron navigated around the tents. Were they glowing because of how the moonlight hit the white fabric? Or because of the incandescent numbers on each one? Whoever had set them up had left several feet of space between each of them.

"I can understand why you joined this club."

"Can you?" Amusement colored his voice. "Why?"

"They have imagination."

He'd joined this club because his parents weren't members, but he'd go with her answer.

Mackenzie squeezed his side. "What do you think is inside each tent?"

He kept his voice droll. "A clown?"

She mock-shuddered. "Seriously. What's your guess?"

"We'll find out in a minute." He parked beside the tent that had their number, hurrying around to help her out. She stepped onto the grass and yelped.

"What is it?" Was she hurt? He ran his eyes down her body. She clutched his forearms.

"Maybe too much imagination. My heels are sinking."

He smirked. "Well, this night keeps getting better and better."

She pressed her lips together. "For you."

She nibbled the corner of her mouth, eyes darting between the cart and the tent.

"And you as well." He swept her into his arms. She fit as if made for him. "Oh yes, better than dancing."

She looped her arms around his neck and he forgot what he was supposed to be doing. Her perfume wrapped around them until his lungs filled with the scent of her.

"Mackenzie." He rested his forehead against hers. "How close are we to step thirteen?"

* * *

Mackenzie lifted the flap of the tent and he ducked under. Two low burgundy couches sat before a low center table. Small lamps provided lighting and soft music played from tiny speakers. A bouquet of roses scented the air.

"Oh. This is beautiful."

He had to agree. "Beautiful." He caressed her face with his eyes.

"You can put me down."

His hands clenched, resisting the idea. "I don't want to."

"Cameron." She brushed a finger down his cheek. He closed his eyes, savoring her touch.

Was she the woman he was supposed to spend his life with? He wanted her to be his Proverbs 31 woman.

He placed her gently on one couch and knelt at her feet. "Let me help you." He unbuckled the straps of her shoes. "This way you can't damage any more of the golf course."

"Ha-ha."

He grinned and sat at the opposite end of the couch, pulling her legs onto his lap.

"I wonder what's happening in the other tents."

He smirked. "I'm sure we don't want to know." He tipped his chin to the transparent roof. "I'd rather take a moment to marvel at God's handiwork."

Thirty-One

Chapter 31

She wasn't sure how Cameron knew their food had arrived, but he did. He adjusted her legs and lifted the flap to collect the tray someone had left there.

Mackenzie scooted to one side of the sofa. She stared at the heavens, contemplating his words.

"Do you believe the Magi would have followed the star if they'd lived in our time?"

Cameron handed her a bowl of soup, which she cradled as she waited for his answer. He reclaimed his seat, balancing his own bowl. He took a sip and encouraged her to do the same.

Hmm. The cream of pumpkin soup was delicious.

"I don't know that they would have noticed the star if they'd lived in our time."

She kept her eyes on his, sipping her soup as she waited for the rest of his answer.

"We spend so much time distracted by the goals set by

ourselves or others that we have little time for contemplation. And when we have a few spare moments, we bury our faces in a device or our vice of choice."

The reality Cameron described could apply to anyone, regardless of their income bracket.

She scraped the bottom of the bowl. "I'm happy God sent Jesus when He did."

Cameron handed her a plate of appetizers arranged around a small white sauce cup. She dipped a cocktail patty into the dark brown condiment. Her eyes widened at the pop of sweet and savory flavors that danced on her tongue.

"Hmm. Okay, these people get my vote." Her lips curved. "I may need the recipe to take back to Orange Valley."

He chuckled. She loved his laugh. The deep, throaty sound made her want to say more outrageous things, to hear it again.

"I'm glad you came to the ball with me." He made a face. "Things didn't quite turn out how I'd hoped, but I intend to get you back to Orange Valley for Christmas. I'm sure you wish to spend time with Madison."

She squirmed at the flicker of guilt. She hadn't thought of her twin once today. Or about how strange Madison had acted the last time they'd spoken. Cameron had consumed all her thoughts.

"Mackenzie?"

"Sorry." She shook her head and rested the plate on the ground, appetite gone.

"Where did you go?"

Concern filled his gray eyes. Should she tell him what was going on with her sister? She considered how he'd responded to her despair over Madison's barrenness. How he'd comforted her. This was a man she could trust with her most precious secrets, maybe even her heart.

"Something's going on with Madison. I'm not sure what." She told him about the child in the background and her sister's early morning call from a kitchen that was not hers.

"What if she's in trouble?" Shouldn't the famous twin's intuition tell her if her sister was in danger?

Cameron caught her hands in his. "We'll be with her tomorrow. Promise. In fact," he scooted closer to her. "Let's pray for her."

Tears filled her eyes. "You want to pray for my sister?"

"Of course." He cleared his throat. "I care about you, Mackenzie. That means I care what happens to the people who are important to you."

She slid closer and hugged him. "Thank you." She shifted back a few inches and held out her hands. "I'm ready."

Cameron clasped her hands and closed his eyes. She did the same.

"Abba Father, we lift Madison up before You. We're not sure what's happening with her, but we're thankful You do. If she's in danger, protect her.

"If she needs help, rescue her. Please soothe Mackenzie's worries and get us safely back to Orange Valley tomorrow so we can confirm that she's okay. In Your name, we pray. Amen."

"Thank you."

The words slipped past trembling lips. He'd prayed for her and had sensed her worry about her sister and accepted them as his own. Was it surprising she'd fallen in love with him?

* * *

Mackenzie slid into a pew with Cameron. When he'd asked her

to attend a midnight service with him, the answer had been yes. How could it have been anything else after he'd shouldered her burden as his own?

The small church was hushed as everyone's attention zeroed in on the platform. Men and women performed an interpretive dance of the nativity story. The music was beautiful and haunting.

What had it been like for Mary and Joseph that long ago night as they waited for their baby to be born?

Cameron leaned closer to her. "Beautiful, isn't it?"

She nodded, too entranced by the performance to speak. Being the earthly parents of the Son of God had been a formidable responsibility. Had Mary and Joseph felt like imposters as they taught Jesus to speak? To take care of Himself? About the love of God?

Had they speculated about how their family would affect the world? After all, they'd known the Messianic prophecies. Had they recognized that through Christ, all the families of the world would be blessed?

Was that why family was important to God? Because it was the unit He used to pass on instructions? The community where individuals learned to love each other and Him. Was that why it was important for Cameron to understand what a family was?

Or maybe it had nothing to do with Cameron and everything to do with her.

She glanced at Cameron. His eyes were on the performers, emotion dancing over his face. She was glad they'd taken off their masks, so she was free to study every inch of his face.

This man had shown up in her world and revealed pieces of himself she doubted he'd ever shared with anyone else. He'd walked with her as she sought to bring order to her family's business.

Two weeks ago, if someone had suggested she'd fall in love with Cameron Grant, she'd have scoffed. The man was so far out of her league he needed his own country code. But weren't they both God's children? Hadn't God grafted both of them into His family?

If God didn't hold a person's financial status against them, why should she?

She'd been asking him to separate himself from his upbringing and his wealth because it made her uncomfortable. It made her feel like an imposter.

But if Cameron could accept her, someone who was beneath him in social and financial status, then she could accept all of him, too.

She rested a hand on top of his, smiling when he shifted until their palms were together. She sighed and rested her head against his shoulder. He was a safe place for her. Family. If only she had the perfect words to express it to him—without sounding weird, or coming across as a pathetic gold digger.

Thirty-Two

Chapter 32

Mackenzie sat in the passenger seat, her leg jigging faster the nearer they got to her house. Her agitation was making him nervous. Didn't they claim twins knew when their sibling was in danger? Was Madison in trouble?

Please, Lord, keep Madison safe.

Mackenzie opened the door before he came to a complete stop.

"Hey."

She whipped her head to glare at him. He lifted his hands and kept his voice calm. "I get that you're worried about your sister—"

"My twin." She snapped out the words.

"I know you're worried about Madison. But going into the house agitated is not the best thing. What if there's nothing wrong?"

She narrowed her eyes and opened her mouth to retort. He spoke fast.

"If something *is* wrong, your agitation will make it worse."

He held her gaze, praying she'd hear the wisdom in his words. After a long moment, she sighed, shoulders sagging.

"You're right." She took a few deep breaths. "She's already been through so much."

He nodded, though he didn't quite understand how Madison felt about not being able to have children. Maybe someday she'd be open to considering other alternatives.

"It will be alright, Princess." He took Mackenzie's hands in his, warming the icy fingers between his palms. "God is always with your sister, even when you can't be there with her."

Her lips trembled. "How do you always know what to say?"

Cameron shrugged. He didn't, but he'd been praying for Madison since last night. He had to believe God was for them and was working things out for their good.

"Let's check on your sister."

Cameron followed Mackenzie inside as she unlocked the front door.

"Madison?" Mackenzie called as she hurried through the entry hall.

He closed the door and studied the pictures, giving Mackenzie space to reunite with her sister. He tuned out the low hum of their voices, not wanting to eavesdrop. After what felt like an hour but was only about ten minutes, the voices got louder.

He turned to observe Mackenzie and Madison together. They were remarkably similar. Some would say mirror images. Yet Cameron identified tiny differences between them. There was a shadow in Madison's eyes—those troubles Mackenzie hinted at had left a mark. Madison's face was also a shade rounder than Mackenzie's.

Madison's eyes widened when she recognized him. "What is he doing here?" She whipped her head to stare at Mackenzie. "Did he follow you?" She clutched her sister's hand.

"It's okay," Mackenzie spoke in a soothing voice. "Cameron and I are together." She gave him a soft smile over her shoulder. One that teased an answering one from him. Was it too soon to ask her to be his wife?

"What do you mean 'together'?" Madison frowned as her gaze flitted from him to Mackenzie. Her eyes widened. "You mean *together* together?"

Mackenzie nodded, the corner of her mouth curving.

"*He's* the mystery guy?" Madison's voice was almost a shriek.

What was she talking about? Was he the mystery guy? If Mackenzie and her sister were talking about him, then maybe he had a shot at forever with her.

Mackenzie snuck a peek at him and nodded. His chest swelled. He was the mystery guy. Wait. The implications of the phrase hit him. She hadn't told her sister about him? Maybe this wasn't as serious for her as it was for him.

"Mackenzie," he gestured to the door behind him. "I'm going to—"

"No," she bolted across the room and snatched his hand. "You can't leave. You're spending Christmas Day with me and Madison."

"Not me." Madison shook her head. "I have plans."

"What do you mean?"

Madison shifted from one foot to the next. "I'm having dinner with a friend."

Cameron suspected Madison had a date, but Mackenzie didn't pick up on it. Instead, Mackenzie gaped at her sister.

"You made plans without me?"

Madison's gaze darted away from Mackenzie's. "I didn't expect you to come back to Orange Valley for Christmas."

Mackenzie's voice was soft. "We always spend Christmas together."

"I know, but—"

"I checked out of a penthouse suite and took a flight to be here with you."

Madison's eyebrows winged up, and she cast a speculative glance at him.

"Well," Madison tilted her chin, reminding him of Mackenzie as she'd faced down his mother. "I didn't ask you to. I have plans and I can't change them."

"Okay," Mackenzie shrugged. "We'll come with you."

Fear flashed across Madison's face. She was hiding something. He was sure of it. Was this what had triggered Mackenzie's apprehension about her sister?

"You can't." Madison's voice trembled.

"Why not?" Mackenzie folded her arms across her chest.

"It's a small house party. Tiny." Madison held her thumb and forefinger a smidgen apart, still refusing to make eye contact. "You can't come."

Hurt radiated off Mackenzie.

"Princess," he turned her to face him, kept both hands on her shoulders. "It would be an honor to spend Christmas with you."

Tears shimmered in her eyes as she looked at him. "Are you sure you don't want to go home?"

You're my home. He almost said the words.

"Are you trying to get rid of me?"

He'd wanted to spend the day with her, though he'd have

preferred if it had happened without her being hurt. Cameron glanced at Madison. She stared at Mackenzie, arms wrapped around herself. Whatever she was hiding, she hadn't enjoyed hurting her sister.

"What would we do?" Mackenzie recaptured his attention.

"We'll figure something out."

What was the good of having money if you couldn't use it to make the woman you loved happy?

"Okay." She stepped closer and slipped her arms around his waist.

Madison met his eyes over Mackenzie's head. "Thank you." She mouthed the words. He nodded, though he hadn't done it for her. He'd do anything for Mackenzie. Now he needed to come up with something that would take her mind off her sister's defection.

Thirty-Three

Chapter 33

Madison tucked several wrapped packages into a large tote bag. This wasn't an impersonal house party as her sister had pretended. Madison put the bulging bag beside the front door and veered toward the kitchen. Mackenzie followed her.

"Who did you say was hosting the party?"

This was her community and while she wasn't familiar with everyone, maybe the hostess was a friend.

"You don't know him as he recently moved into town." Madison pulled items from the cupboard and refrigerator, putting them in a large shopping bag.

Mackenzie's eyebrows winged up. "Him?"

Madison had met someone? Was there something wrong with him? Was that why Madison was hiding their relationship?

"Them. They're new in town. You wouldn't have met them."

Mackenzie laid a hand on her sister's arm. "Emmy, what's going on?"

Madison laughed, the sound as fake as the tinsel on Christmas trees.

"Nothing." Madison's eyes shifted away from hers.

"You're lying. You never keep secrets from me." Hurt colored her voice. Madison met her gaze and clutched her arm.

"I'm sorry. I'll tell you everything as soon as I can."

So she *was* hiding something. Why couldn't Madison share it with her? Mackenzie swallowed the rest of her words and nodded.

"Please don't be mad." Madison threw her arms around Mackenzie's waist and squeezed. "I need time to work some things out." Madison rested her head on Mackenzie's shoulder. She sighed and hugged her sister back. As much as she wanted to keep asking questions until she'd uncovered all of Madison's secrets, she wouldn't. She'd follow Cameron's lead and pray for her sister, trusting God to take care of her.

She had to release Madison into God's hands. It wouldn't be easy because Mackenzie had spent a lifetime protecting her sister. Though Madison had been born seven minutes before Mackenzie, it had always been that way.

Madison was impulsive and rushed into things. Mackenzie would go in and smooth things over. It would have to stop. She kissed her sister's forehead.

Lord, I release Madison into Your hands. Please take care of her.

"Besides," Madison pulled away. "You can't tell me you're not happy to spend time with the handsome billionaire." She threw a glance over her shoulder as if she expected Cameron to walk in while they were talking about him. "Isn't he a client?"

Mackenzie pressed her palms to her warm cheeks. "Yes. No."

She shook her head. Madison wasn't the only twin keeping secrets. Cameron was more to her than a handsome man. He was the man she'd fallen in love with and wanted to spend the rest of her life with.

She was such a hypocrite. Here she was, getting angry because Madison had a secret when she had one of her own. Madison waited patiently, probably sensing the turmoil in her heart.

Mackenzie flicked a glance over her shoulder. "I think I love him, Em."

Madison arched a brow. "Think?"

Her laugh had a tinge of hysteria. "Okay. I'm sure. I'm utterly and completely in love with Cameron Grant."

Madison's eyes widened, snagged on something beyond her shoulder. Mackenzie froze. She smothered a groan and turned.

Cameron stood in the doorway, shock etched on his face. Why hadn't she checked before she'd made her big confession? Better yet, why hadn't she kept her mouth shut?

"I'll leave you guys to talk." Madison crammed a few more items into the bulging shopping bag before hustling out of the kitchen.

Neither of them moved until the front door slammed. Mackenzie jolted and began buzzing around the kitchen.

"Well, we have a lot to do if we're going to have any Christmas dinner." She opened the cupboard, staring at the contents, but not seeing a thing. Maybe he hadn't heard what she said. Or he may have misunderstood. Cameron came up behind her.

"Mackenzie."

She darted away, intending to open the fridge. He must consider her the most foolish woman on earth—falling in love after a few weeks.

"Mackenzie." His voice was more urgent. She shut her eyes. She'd never work as a hostess again. How could she, when everything would remind her of him?

She gulped in a deep breath, almost sighing when the scent of sunshine filled her lungs. She had to get out of here, needed space so she could think and breathe without his delicious scent messing with her head.

"Mackenzie. Why are you running away from me?" Cameron placed his large hands on her shoulders, turning her gently to him.

She couldn't look at him. The whole time they'd kept this thing between them light and easy. It was one thing to say they were in a relationship. Falling in love made things complicated. Especially when it was one-sided.

"Kenzie?" He cupped her chin. "Can you look at me? Please?"

She took a deep breath and met his gray eyes. Emotions swirled in their depths, but without a key to decipher them, she was clueless.

"Did you mean what you said?"

She pretended to misunderstand. "I said a lot of things. What are you talking about specifically?"

Please don't let him mention her confession.

"Specifically, when you said you were completely and utterly in love with me."

He caressed her cheek. She closed her eyes, savoring the sensation of his hand against her skin. She would miss having Cameron's full attention. This close to him, she could lay her head on his chest. Curl her arms around him.

"Did you mean it?"

His gruff voice seemed to echo in the room. What was she doing? She wasn't a coward. If this was their last moment together, then he should know how she felt about him. She drew in a breath, pressed her shoulders back, and met his gaze.

"Yes, Cameron. I'm in love with you."

"Finally!"

Her eyes widened. "I beg your pardon?"

He stepped closer, reducing the gap between them to a hairsbreadth.

"Finally." He cradled her face in his hands. "I've been waiting for you to catch up. Because I am utterly and completely in love with you, Mackenzie Noelle Porter."

He was? Her eyes flicked between his, searching for the truth. The expression in his eyes convinced her. Cameron was in love with her. A grin stole over her face. He loved her.

She looped her arms around his neck. "This is where we kiss."

"Is it?" His thumb grazed her cheek.

"Hmm-mph. You love me and I love you. This is the part of every romance where they kiss."

"Well, we wouldn't want to skip any steps."

"Of course not."

He continued to caress her face, eyes filled with emotion.

"Pretty sure this is not how people kiss."

The last time his lips had met hers, it had almost blasted off the top of her head. But this? The heat swirling in his eyes, his tender caress…it was enough to have her melt into a puddle.

"MyKenzie." He kissed the corner of her mouth. "I'm glad we're finally on the same step." He kissed the other side of her mouth.

"Uhm?"

What were they talking about? Why were they still talking?

"Cameron." She may have growled his name. She wasn't

sure. "Is there something I can do to direct your kiss to my lips?"

He chuckled. "No. I'm taking my time. I only get to kiss you once after the first time you tell me you are in love with me."

He kissed the tip of her nose. "My Kenzie. I love you."

He brushed his lips against hers in the lightest of kisses. Though she'd braced herself for it, the passion that rushed through her made her suck in a breath. Would every kiss be this mind-blowing? Cameron changed the angle of his head, deepening the kiss.

Oh, my word. She never wanted to kiss anyone else for the rest of her life. Cameron was it for her. She used her lips to communicate what words hadn't quite been able to express.

She loved him and wanted to spend the rest of her life with him. She was grateful God had convinced him to follow her after she'd run away. Because, aside from salvation, being with Cameron was the best gift she'd ever received.

Thirty-Four

Chapter 34

Cameron parked on the street in front of a pale yellow house with white trimmings. He turned to grin at Mackenzie. She loved him.

"You're pleased with yourself."

He smirked, lifting a hand to play with the hair she'd left loose around her shoulders. "I am. The girl I've been crushing on likes me back."

"Hmm." She ran her fingers over his eyebrow. "What's not to like? You're a remarkably handsome man."

He grinned. "This is about my looks?"

"Yes." Her eyes dropped to his lips. "And your kisses." Her words came out breathy. "I adore your kisses."

He shifted, leaning closer to her. "Maybe we should stock up. We have a long day ahead and no opportunities to kiss."

"Unless they have mistletoe."

"Suppose they don't." He arched a brow in challenge. "Is that a risk you're willing to take?"

"You're right." She wrapped her arms around his neck. "Better make it a good one."

His mouth was an inch away from hers when someone rapped on the passenger door. His head snapped toward the unwelcome sound. Levi grinned at him and he groaned. His friend had the worst timing.

"Give me a minute. My friend is about to have an accident."

Mackenzie laughed. "It's okay, CJ. We'll have lots of time for kisses later."

He stole a kiss—a mere brush of his lips against hers, not the full-on, passionate one he'd been after. "I look forward to it."

He hopped out of the truck, rushing around to get Mackenzie's door for her. He was apprehensive about introducing Mackenzie and Levi. Levi was his oldest friend—his only friend. Would the two of them get along?

"Mackenzie, this is Levi." Cameron kept his arm around her, needing to have her close to him.

Levi narrowed his eyes at her. "Miss, is this guy bothering you? I have friends who are police officers. I'd be happy to ensure he gets what's coming to him."

"Uh," Mackenzie's eyes darted between him and Levi, brow furrowed, "is there a joke I'm missing out on?"

Trust her to pick up on that. He massaged the back of his neck. "I may have told him I was stalking an employee."

A secretive smile teased the corner of her lips as her gaze met his. "Best stalker ever."

His eyes dropped to her lips. "Yeah?"

Levi groaned. "Let's get you two into the house where there are lots of people lest you forget you're saved." Levi gave Mackenzie a hard stare. "You are a believer, right?"

"Yes." Mackenzie met Levi's gaze with a soft smile.

The man was exasperating. Still, Cameron didn't hold it against him. He and Levi were brothers of the heart. Levi held out a hand to Mackenzie.

"Let me introduce you to everyone. Cam, Mom said you're to come see her as soon as you get here. She's in the kitchen."

Levi tucked Mackenzie's arms into his and strolled away.

"Why don't you get your own girl?" Cameron shouted after Levi without the tiniest bit of heat. Mackenzie was safer with Levi and his family than she'd been around his and she'd survived a run-in with his mother. Cameron shook his head and went to answer his summons.

Louise Armstrong's head lifted the second he stepped into the warm kitchen.

"It's about time you got here."

The scent of pot-roasted beef and fragrant rice and peas filled the air. Cameron drew in a long breath. He would enjoy today's meal.

He grinned. "I had to time it until dinner was almost ready."

Anna, Levi's sister-in-law, and her daughter Avery turned toward him.

"Uncle Cameron." Avery abandoned the cucumbers she was slicing under her mother's eagle eye. She threw her arms around him. "I'm glad you're here. Grandma Louise was hoping you'd come this year."

Shame pulsed through him. He needed to do better at visiting Louise and Earl. The couple had opened their home to him many times. They'd called him every week after his baptism to encourage his faith.

The calls had tapered off when he'd taken over the running of his family's company. But he could still count on a call for every major milestone—birthdays or any major project he spearheaded. There was even the occasional check-in to make sure he was doing okay.

"Well?" Louise plopped her hands on her hips. "Don't I get a hug?"

"Hey, Anna." He smiled at the petite woman before stepping further into the room.

"Mama Louise." He hugged her, enjoying the scent of fruit cake that clung to her skin. "Merry Christmas."

"It would be merrier if you'd drop by more often."

"I'm sorry." He kissed the top of her head. "You can always visit me in Portsville. I'd send the plane for you."

She pulled away. "Boy, what do I know about flying in planes?"

It was her standard response. She opened a pot on the stove, amplifying the scent of roasted beef that permeated the air.

"I'll try to visit more often." He'd be flying down to see Mackenzie, anyway. He could convince her to spend some time with the Armstrongs.

Louise studied him. "Found a girl, did you? It's about time."

"He stalked an employee, Mom." Levi strode into the room. "Surely that should count for something?" Levi hugged his niece, one arm snaking around to sneak a cucumber slice from the cutting board.

"I'm more concerned about when you're going to find a girl. You're not getting any younger." Louise pretended to glare at her son.

"Look what you've done." Levi glowered at him. "We were supposed to be united in our singleness."

Cameron shrugged. "What can I say? When love comes calling, you'd better answer."

Louise and Anna beamed at him. Avery giggled.

"Uncle Cameron, you sound like one of those guys in those movies Mom's always watching."

"That's because he's in love, dear." Anna smiled at Avery before nodding at him. "She must be wonderful if she won Cameron's heart."

Speaking of…Cameron arched a brow at Levi. "Where's Mackenzie?"

"She's in the backyard with Pops and Aaron. She may have ousted me from my spot behind the grill."

"Oh?" Cameron's eyebrow winged up.

"Yeah." Levi snatched another cucumber slice. "She's out there whipping up some 'magic sauce' she claims will make the jerked chicken the best we've ever eaten."

"Good." Anna gave Levi a sly glance. "Maybe she'll convince Aaron to remove the meat before they turn into charcoal."

Everyone laughed. Aaron loved using the grill but would get caught up in conversations and forget to remove the food in time. The result was meat that was dry and chewy.

Cameron sighed with relief. He'd worried that Mackenzie wouldn't fit in among his friends.

Thank You, God.

Only his Heavenly Father could have directed him to the woman who was a perfect fit in every aspect of his life.

Thirty-Five

Chapter 35

Mackenzie's sides hurt from a combination of too much food and laughter. The Armstrongs had welcomed her and tucked her within the folds of their family, accepting her as one of their own. She'd eaten more than her fair share of food, savoring each delicious mouthful.

After dinner, they lingered around the table, telling stories about their family. Cameron's name came up almost as often as Levi's and Aaron's.

Though they didn't share the same blood, this was Cameron's family. His smile came easier here as he settled in among people who loved him, no questions asked.

"You should come for the scavenger hunt tomorrow, Mackenzie." Anna's soft words grabbed everyone's attention.

"Yes." Earl assented. "We'll print a sheet for you and Cameron."

Mackenzie's head flipped back and forth between the eager faces. She wanted to agree, to spend more time with this family, but how could she? She and Cameron had made no plans after today. Would he still be in town? Was this a Christmas romance, or was there hope for more?

Cameron grabbed her hand under the table. "We should come. It's been a while since I've done one, but they're always fun."

"Okay."

The corner of her mouth curved. Had she ever smiled this much in one day? Genuine smiles that came from the depths of her heart? Instead of worrying about the future, she'd take it one day at a time and trust God. If He'd brought Cameron into her life, He must have a plan for what came next.

* * *

"There." Mackenzie pointed through the windscreen. "A For Sale sign."

When she'd agreed to a scavenger hunt, she'd expected to be hunting for things like rocks and leaves of a certain color as she had as a child. Instead, she and Cameron had been driving around town, searching for the strangest things. A statue to shake hands with. A fire hydrant. Cat.

Some things were simple enough to find. The trick sometimes was taking a picture with yourself and the item. The cat hadn't appreciated Mackenzie's attempt to take a photo with it and had yowled and scratched. If not for the additional layers because of the day's chill, she'd have had scrapes on her arms.

Cameron parked, and the two of them hurried to get a selfie in front of the sign. She snuggled under his arms, grateful for the chance to be close to him. Cameron snapped the picture and tucked the phone in his pocket.

"This is too perfect a moment to pass up."

"What?"

He turned her in his arms and brushed the tips of his fingers across her cheeks. "Perfect."

He pressed his lips to hers and she sighed, allowing herself a moment to enjoy the sweetness of his kiss before pulling away.

"We have a few more things to find."

His arms tightened around her. "I surrender."

She quirked a brow. "You concede victory to Levi and Avery?"

Cameron rolled his eyes. "When you put it that way," he dropped his arms and slid his fingers between hers. "I refuse to be beaten by a five-year-old girl."

She bit back a smile. "I'm offended. Does it bother you because it's a girl or because she's young?"

"Because it's Avery. She makes up songs and dances as she collects her prize." His lips quirked. "Levi sends me videos. Here," he fished out his phone and pulled up a video. "This is from last year."

The little girl had a gift. Though the words of her song were nonsensical, her dance moves were on point, mimicking the steps from a popular music video.

"You're right." She mock-shuddered. "We can't become the next target of Avery's parodies. What do we have left on the list?"

Cameron angled the sheet of paper so she could scan it.

"Okay," Mackenzie pointed to an item on the list, "if we go into the town square, we can take a photo beside the Christmas tree."

"Maybe there will be a store with a wreath on the door?"

"And then we can get ice cream and take a picture of us eating it."

"Okay." Cameron checked his watch. "If we separate, we can get the job done in half the time."

"Genius." She stood on tip-toe and kissed his cheek.

"That's the wrong spot." He reached for her.

She danced out of reach. "Oh no, you won't distract me with any more of those lethal kisses."

"Lethal? You think my kisses are lethal?" He opened her door before hopping in.

"Yup." She buckled her seatbelt. "They're dangerous to my peace of mind."

* * *

The hunt for a Christmas wreath was more challenging than she'd expected. She found lights, bells, bows, tiny Christmas trees...no wreath. Where would she find a wreath in this town?

Ruby's Place. Of course, she almost laughed aloud. Ruby always had a wreath on her door for the holidays. She hurried to the restaurant and snapped a photo before dashing away.

She'd been gone a long time. Cameron was probably already back at the car and her ice cream had melted into a gooey mess—not her favorite way to enjoy the frozen treat. She sent a text to Cameron. Got it.

Cameron: On my way to you.

She stepped up her pace, swerving to avoid bumping into a lanky man hurrying toward her.

"Mackenzie?"

"Yes?" She paused mid-stride, scanning the bearded man

from the tips of his boots to the plaid shirt under his brown leather jacket.

"What are you doing here?" His lips tipped up in a smile that transformed his face from ordinary to good-looking.

"Uhm," she pointed over her shoulder. "Scavenger hunt."

Did she know him? Maybe they'd met on a flight. Or in one of the many cities she'd visited.

"Do you want to hang out for a few hours? No chaperone." His smile was a little too intimate.

She backed away. "Uh, no." She waggled her fingers. "Nice seeing you again." Maybe if she hurried, he wouldn't realize she hadn't referred to him by name.

True to his word, Cameron was on his way to meet her. She ran toward him, burying her face in his chest, aware that the stranger still watched her.

"Hey," Cameron pulled back to study her face. "Is everything alright?"

"It is now."

She glanced behind her. The man scowled, hands balling into fists before he stalked away. She sagged against Cameron in relief. Determined not to let her lingering disquiet ruin the rest of the day with Cameron, she tucked the incident into the back of her mind.

"Didn't want you to eat all my ice cream."

His eyes darted between hers. "Are you sure that's it?"

"What do you mean?"

He cradled her face. "You know this is the beginning for us, right?"

She gulped. Why did he have to bring up the one topic she was trying not to worry about?

"It's okay if it doesn't work out for us." It would have to be.

Cameron scowled. "Did you hear me when I told you I loved you?"

"Yes, but we live in different cities. How—?" She bit off the rest of the words because they hurt too much to consider.

"I'm not sure how that's going to work out yet, but you're important to me, Mackenzie. I make time for the things—and people—who matter to me."

"Okay," she mustered up a smile. "We'll talk about that later."

"No. Even being shamed by a five-year-old won't make me rush this conversation. I love you, MyKenzie. This is not a holiday romance for me. It's the real deal. The type that has me pondering wedding rings and relocation."

Her eyes widened. "Wedding rings?"

He lifted a brow. "Too soon?" He kissed the tip of her nose. "I'm still waiting for you to give me a list of those steps."

"You're doing fine on your own." She frowned. "Why do you call me My Kenzie?"

"Because that's what I want you to be—My Mackenzie. The woman I come home to. The love of my life. My family."

Her eyes stung with tears. "That's what I want too."

Why was she worrying about the future? Hadn't God already shown her He had all her tomorrows in His hand? Who but God could have redeemed one of the most embarrassing moments of her life to grant her the love she'd always dreamed of?

"Good. What do you say we leave the future in God's hands and focus on this moment?"

His words echoed her thoughts—confirmation of God's hand in their story.

"Brilliant plan." She tugged his head down to hers. "This is another one of those kissing moments."

"Happy to oblige." His lips met hers and Mackenzie forgot about everything except Cameron. The man who loved her as completely as she loved him.

Epilogue

Madison stifled the swell of envy. Mackenzie and Cameron snuggled on the couch, ignoring the Hallmark movie that played on the screen. And why not? They were having their own real-life romance.

Mackenzie and Cameron were so in love that it hurt to be around them, especially since she'd had a shot at her own once-in-a-lifetime love and messed it up. All because she'd kept secrets.

The envy changed to guilt. Secrets even her twin was unaware of. Maybe she should return to Cinnamon Hill. The reminders of all she had lost were everywhere in Orange Valley. How could she remain here?

But first, she'd confess everything to Mackenzie. Explain why she'd been adamant they switch places, and all that had happened while she'd been pretending to be Mackenzie.

Yes. She'd tell Mackenzie everything. Tomorrow. She turned away from the happy couple, not wanting to bring the cloud of her sadness into the room and mar their happiness.

"Madison, come sit with us," Mackenzie called before she made her escape. "You're supposed to be watching this movie with us."

Madison dredged up a smile for her sister, the one she pulled out for special occasions. Like when someone asked for the thousandth time when she planned to have children and she wanted to scream.

"The movie you're *not* watching?"

Madison gestured to the credits rolling on the screen. Her sister and Cameron exchanged sheepish glances. Oh. She was the worst sister ever. Mackenzie deserved this slice of happiness. She would be happy for her sister. Even if it meant pushing her own sadness down to the bottom of her feet.

"We may have gotten a little distracted," Cameron admitted with a smile for Mackenzie. "But we'll do better." His gray eyes met hers and for a second, she wondered if he'd been able to discern her secrets. He shifted away from her sister. "You sit here." He patted the space between him and Mackenzie.

"Hey," Mackenzie pouted. "That's my spot."

"I know, Princess. But without some distance between us, even your sister can't prevent me from stealing a kiss."

"Oh, I'm the chaperone." Madison mock-glared.

Cameron stroked his chin. "That's one way to consider it. Or you can use this as an opportunity to find out everything you can about the guy your sister's dating."

She stomped over to the couch and flopped down between them, feigning anger. Her uncharitable feelings had dissipated. He was right. This was a chance to learn if he was as wonderful as he appeared. Mackenzie had always looked out for her. This was her chance to take care of her sister for a change.

"If you insist on forcing me into the role of a chaperone, I intend to ask the most embarrassing questions."

Cameron chuckled. "Ask away. I have no secrets from

Mackenzie."

If only she could say the same.

* * *

Madison has a secret—a big one. Can she tell the truth in time to get the family she always dreamed of? Or will the truth cause everything to crumble to smithereens? Find out in A Family for Christmas.

* * *

Did you enjoy Mackenzie and Cameron's story? Sign up for my newsletter at https://tinyurl.com/AHFCBonus and get a bonus epilogue.

Author's Note

Thank you for reading Cameron and Mackenzie's story. I had so much fun writing this book!

I'm fascinated with twins, and so, when I decided to write a Christmas novella, I chose a twin switch.

I always enjoyed those stories where twins switch places and something magical happens. I wanted to play with that a little, which is why Cameron knew from the beginning that something was off.

The theme of family is strong in this book because each of us was born or placed into a unit where we don't always fit. Sometimes, it can be difficult if your family is not the type you want to spend Christmas with.

A Husband for Christmas is a reminder that family goes deeper than the people we share DNA with.

Our Heavenly Father has grafted those who accept Jesus as their Lord and Savior into His family. This is such a stunning idea that I want you to sit with that thought for a minute.

The Bible uses powerful language when it talks about those who are in God's family.

- Romans 11:11-31 says God has grafted us into His family.
- Ephesians 1:5 says God has adopted us.

Grafting is an intricate process where two different things are fused into one. When a graft is successful, a new thing results, and they cannot separate the two without damage to them both.

An adoption is a legal process where unrelated people become part of the same family. The adopter chooses the adoptee (and, in some cases, the reverse is also true).

God adopted you and grafted you into His family. So whether you have a fabulous earthly family or one that makes you cringe, I hope you'll remember that, especially during the holidays.

See how very much our Father loves us, for he calls us his children, and that is what we are! (1 John 3:1) God loves you, my friend. Take comfort in that.

If you enjoyed this novella, please consider leaving a review online as this helps get the book to other readers who'll enjoy it as you did.

About the Author

Aminata Coote's love affair with books began with an upside-down copy of Silas Marner. She's passionate about helping women understand the truth of the Bible for themselves.

She writes stories and books that point to a God bigger than our failings and provide hope to others. Aminata is also the author of several Bible studies and devotionals.

She lives in Montego Bay, Jamaica with her husband and son.

Connect with her on her website, aminatacoote.com, or on Instagram or Facebook @aminatacoote. Learn more about her books at https://aminatacoote.com/books-by-aminata-coote/.

Sign up for Aminata's newsletter at https://tinyurl.com/FreeReadingJournal for a free reading journal.

Other Books by the Author

Inspirational Contemporary Romance

Orange Valley
His Perfect Wife
His Perfect Match
His Perfect Family
His Perfect Choice

Christmas with the Porters
A Husband for Christmas
A Family for Christmas

The Firefighters of Orange Valley
Falling For Her Fake Wedding Date

Christian Living
Face Your Fear: Choose Faith Over Fear
Affirmations for Christian Women: Biblical Affirmations for
Spiritual and Emotional Self-Care
7 Lessons on Endurance from Hebrews 12:1-2

Through God's Eyes: Marriage Lessons for Women
Unwavering: How to Stand Strong in Your Faith

Learn more about my books at
https://tinyurl.com/ACooteBooks

Newsletter Sign-up

Sign Up for Aminata's Newsletter

What happens when Cameron and Mackenzie get to step thirteen?

Join Aminata's mailing list at https://tinyurl.com/AHFCBonus to read the bonus epilogue of *A Husband for Christmas*.

Join Aminata's community

Website: https://aminatacoote.com

Facebook: https://www.facebook.com/AminataCoote

Instagram: https://www.instagram.com/aminatacoote/

Want more inspirational romance?

Check out the Orange Valley series.

His Perfect Wife

First love, second chances: Can they mend a broken heart?

Tonya McPherson once dreamed of marrying her first love, but four years after he left her, she's abandoned the idea of a fairy tale ending. Now he's back, and they're forced to work together. Can her heart withstand the constant "what-ifs"?

Malcolm Hall deeply regrets breaking up with Tonya. Assigned as the youth pastor at her church, he yearns for a second chance. Can Tonya find it in her heart to forgive him?

Is it too late for a fresh start, or will they let a once-in-a-lifetime love slip away?

His Perfect Match

Two unlikely lovers, battling financial woes.

Brianna McPherson, a struggling communications consultant, desperately needs paying clients, or her business will crumble.

Daniel Hutchinson's church faces imminent closure unless he can attract new members.

When their paths cross, sparks fly, and an unexpected love blossoms.

In the midst of their professional struggles, they find a love that could change everything.

His Perfect Family

A single mom fighting for her son, a second chance at love.

Gabrielle Wallace is a determined single mother fighting for custody of her son. Theodore McPherson was her first love, the man who'd ghosted her.

Theodore, a firefighter, seeks to make amends for letting Gabrielle go. When he learns she needs a husband to keep her son, he steps up as her groom, hoping to rekindle a lasting love.

Their journey is marked by hurdles and struggles. Can they overcome their past and find happiness together, or will differences tear them apart once more?

His Perfect Choice

She's given up on love, but he's determined to win her heart.

Jessica Smith's dream of being a pastor's wife shatters, testing her faith as she battles Guillain-Barré Syndrome. Her physical therapist, Andre Meyers, harbors years of unspoken love for her and seizes the opportunity to prove it.

Together, they face their past and learn that brokenness can lead to a beautiful future.

In this heartwarming tale of hope, faith, and second chances, will they take a chance on love for their happily ever after?

www.ingramcontent.com/pod-product-compliance
Lightning Source LLC
Chambersburg PA
CBHW020917160726

47993CB00005B/2010